Mucking About

HERE BE GIANTS

THE CAVES of MOAN and GROAN

The DIVIL'S BIT

SLIABH MISHT

HERE BE MOUNTAIN MEN

Manchan's World

ANOTHER HERMIT

Go Away

THE HOLY MOUNTAIN

HERE BE BOARS

The WESTERN EDGE

A WHOLLY WELL

The FAIRY OAK

An Trá

Dun Quarter

DONA DOLI

HERE be VIKINGS

HERE be Jellyfish

SEA SPOUTS

BAH

HERE BE COWPATS

BOG OAK

The Bog of Squelch

CLIFFS of MOHAIR

BALOR'S LEAP

MANCHA ROCK

HERE BE BRAMBLES

HERE BE TURNIPS
THE BOGGY BOG
AN RELIG
ST GRUSACH'S MONASTERY
HERE be WOLVES
DERMOT the HERMIT
Go away
HAG ISLAND
The LAKE of the WORM.
THE LOOP of LOOPS
HERE BE RABBITS
DADDO'S CORACLE
Here be Turnips
e be
BEES
A'S
The Chief's Hut
Manchán's Village
The great Standing Stone
HERE BE NETTLES
Fionn the Stonecutter
The Tangled Forest
Y FORT
LL
THE GAP OF THE BOAR

Mucking About

Being the Adventures of a Boy
living at that Time in Ireland
when the Old Ways were
changing and the New Ones
were just getting started

Written and Illuminated by

John Chambers

Mucking About

First published in 2018 by
Little Island Books
7 Kenilworth Park
Dublin 6W
Ireland

ISBN: 978-1-912417-05-6

Typeset by Gráinne Clear

Cover and inside illustrations by John Chambers

Printed in Poland by Drukarnia Skleniarz

Little Island receives financial assistance from The Arts Council/ An Chomhairle Ealaíon and the Arts Council of Northern Ireland

10 9 8 7 6 5 4 3 2 1

For Charlotte, Ollie, Tess and Enrico

CHAPTER ONE

n which Manchán's Mother tries to force him against his Will to become a Monk. Manchán's Father's three favourite Things. An Introduction to Manchán's annoying Sister Méabh. A Pig called Muck and Pagan-of-the-Six-Toes. A brave Escape.

t was a fine sunny day, and the only dark cloud around was Manchán's face, scowling at his family. For a week now his mother had been hinting at a surprise and at last he had found out what it was. Her brother, the abbot from the monastery across the lake, had come to collect him, for Manchán was going to be sent to become a monk. A *monk* for heaven's sake!

'Don't say that,' said Brother Abstemius.

'Say what?' said Manchán.

'You know what,' said Brother Abstemius, and Manchán sighed.

'Right,' he said. 'Sorry.'

'For your penance,' added Brother Abstemius, 'you shall peel two bushels of turnips for Brother Cook. He needs them for breakfast in the morning.'

Turnips! For breakfast, moaned Manchán, though not out loud. Brother Abstemius was watching

him much too closely for that. Was this how being a monk was going to be?

'There's nothing wrong with monking,' said Manchán's mother, glaring at him. 'It's a very respectable profession. People will look up to you.'

Great, thought Manchán, his mind still reeling from the turnips.

'Is "monking" really a word?' asked Manchán's sister Méabh. 'It doesn't sound like a word to me.'

'Of course it's a word,' said Manchán's father, who couldn't read. 'It's a word like fishing, or hurling, or singing.' He listed off the three things in life that were the most important to him. Now monking was added to the list. 'Good man, Manchán,' he said. 'You'll bring honour to the family.'

Manchán frowned. 'Why can't I bring honour to the family by fishing or hurling or singing?' he asked. 'Like you do.'

His father scratched his head but couldn't come up with an answer. He gave up and waited for Manchán's mother to explain.

'Because,' she said, 'monking is a *respectable* profession.'

'That's it,' replied Manchán's father, nodding. '*Respectable*.' He said the word as if he wasn't quite sure what it meant, which he wasn't.

'It is the *most* respectable profession there is, after chieftain,' said Brother Abstemius modestly, 'and that is something.'

Manchán's mother smiled. Brother Abstemius was her actual brother and had brought much honour to her family with his monking,

as opposed to messing, or mucking about, which Manchán was very good at.

'*Being* a monk,' said Méabh. 'Not *monking*!'

In fact, Brother Abstemius had brought so much honour to Manchán's mother's family that he very nearly made up for her marrying Manchán's father. And now Manchán was about to make up for the rest.

'Anyway, Manchán's good at singing,' continued Méabh, 'and hurling. And two out of three's not bad.'

Thanks, thought Manchán, and blew his cheeks out so hard his ears popped. Things had to be really bad if Méabh was defending him like that. Or maybe she just didn't want him to leave home because there'd be nobody around to bully after he was gone.

'But Manchán's terrible at fishing,' said Méabh. 'Once he caught a hunter from the kingdom across the river on his hook and nearly started a war. Do you want to hear the story?' she said to Brother Abstemius, who looked mildly interested.

'No, he doesn't,' said Manchán. 'So shut up, all right?'

'He hooked him by the seat of his pants,' said Méabh, 'while he was crouching in the reeds, and dragged him into the mud.'

'It wasn't my fault,' said Manchán. 'It was the wind. And you weren't there either, so you don't know!'

Méabh laughed. 'Stop *lying*,' she said. 'You're not allowed to *lie* while you're *monking*. Isn't that true, Brother Abstemius?'

Brother Abstemius's eyebrows wriggled like caterpillars. 'It is true in any case,' he intoned sternly, 'but it is especially true for monks.'

'And what's the penance for lying?' asked Méabh innocently. 'How many bushels of turnips do you have to peel?'

'It depends on the lie,' said Brother Abstemius. 'I work with a scale of one to ten. But go on with the story.'

Manchán sighed. It looked like the stupid story was going to be told whether he liked it or not, and then they would all have a great laugh at his expense. To cheer himself up, he would do his trick of imagining it had happened to somebody else. That would nearly turn it into a good story, except for two things. It didn't happen to somebody else, and these kinds of things were always happening to Manchán.

'It was a fine summer's morning when Manchán set off in his coracle,' Méabh declaimed.

'There wasn't a cloud in the sky and the water was as smooth as Daddy's head.'

'It wasn't always smooth,' said her mother, sighing. 'When I met your father he had hair all

the way down to his waist. And lovely plaits.'

'Aye,' said Daddy, remembering. 'But they were a lot of work.'

'Manchán took the coracle without permission and headed off down to the lake with it,' said Méabh.

'No, I didn't,' said Manchán. 'I asked the day before if I could take the coracle out by myself and Daddy said I could. Didn't you, Daddy?'

'When you were older, is what I said,' his father corrected him.

'But I was older,' said Manchán. 'I was a whole day older.' He glanced over at Brother Abstemius, who was shaking his head and doing his eyebrow wriggle again. You could practically see him counting bushels.

Manchán's mother said, 'This is part of the reason we are sending you to be a monk, Manchán. It will teach you not to stretch the truth. Now, Méabh, you can tell the rest of the story some other time. Manchán has to pack.'

'Wait a second,' said Manchán. 'I thought you were just *discussing* sending me to be a monk. Nobody said you'd made up your minds.'

'Well, we have,' said Manchán's mother, and looked at her husband for support.

'Er …' he said. 'Your mother thinks it will bring honour to our family. And it's just for a year,' he added quickly. 'If you don't like it, we'll think of something else.'

Manchán turned and stamped away. What else can you do when your entire family has turned against you? And the last thing he wanted was for Méabh to see him crying, especially if it was because he was angry, not sad. He stamped into their hut and untied the door so it fell closed behind him. That was the thing about deerskin doors. They kept the wind and the rain out all right, but you couldn't slam them the way you could the wooden ones. But only the chieftains

had wooden doors, and Manchán's father was a very long way away from being a chieftain.

Outside he could hear Brother Abstemius speaking to his mother. 'Don't worry,' he was saying. 'We'll take very good care of Manchán. He'll be settled in no time whatsoever.'

'I'm not a bit worried,' answered Manchán's mother. 'It will do him a lot of good.'

'You're the one who should be worried,' said Méabh. 'Not us.' She gave a short, sharp laugh.

Go on and laugh, thought Manchán bitterly, standing in the middle of the hut. He wiped the tears from his cheeks and waited for his eyes to adjust to the darkness. There were no windows in the hut for light because nobody had invented glass yet, at least nobody local, and a window without glass is just a hole for rain and wind.

'Manchán,' shouted his mother from outside, 'pack your things and get a move on. Brother Abstemius hasn't got all day, you know.'

Manchán started packing. He only had a few things anyway, like most people back then. He

packed them into a bundle and tied it to his
hurley stick. Then he went and quietly kicked
a hole in the wall at the back of the hut. The
hut was built of sods and sticks, so
the wall gave quickly enough and
made hardly any noise. With a bit
of luck, he could make it to the
river and borrow a coracle while
everybody else went haring off in
the wrong direction. *That will show
them*, he thought, getting down on his knees and
widening the hole. Behind him his father's voice
drifted in through the deerskin door.

'You know,' he was saying, '"Honour to the
Family" could be a really great title for a song.'
He started humming like a bee, settling the
tune in his head.

'Why don't you compose the song *after* my
brother has gone?' said Manchán's mother,
interrupting him. Then she raised her voice
again. 'Manchán, what's taking you so long?'

'I'm packing,' shouted Manchán. 'There's no
law against packing, is there?'

The hole was wider now and he could see daylight. *Nearly there*, he thought. *Soon I'll be on my way and then they'll be sorry.* He pressed the palms of his hands together and shoved them forward into the hole like a swimmer practising a dive. He had just managed to force his head through after his hands when Muck appeared.

'Muck,' said Manchán, 'move. You're in the way.'

Muck was Manchán's pig, a small dark pig with pink ears and a tail that wagged like a dog's. He was smarter than a dog too, and followed Manchán everywhere. Now he pressed his snout up against Manchán's nose and grinned at him. Muck loved Manchán. And why wouldn't he? How many other pigs had owners who liked  to grub around in the dirt with them? None, was the answer. Of course he adored the boy.

'Muck,' whispered Manchán, pressing his head forward and trying to twist his shoulders through at the same time, 'I said, get out of the way.'

But Muck just pressed his forehead against Manchán's and started shoving back. He thought the whole thing was a game. Muck loved playing games.

'Muck,' groaned Manchán, because a pig, even a small one, is as solid as a rock and twice as heavy. With his shoulders still pinned, all Manchán was able to do was prod Muck with his fingers to try to get him out of the way, which to Muck was like being tickled.

Wheee wheee wheeee, squealed Muck in delight. Muck loved being tickled.

'Muck, stop squealing,' hissed Manchán, scrabbling with his toes on the floor of the hut behind and getting nowhere fast. 'Somebody will hear you.' By 'somebody', of course, he meant his mother.

'You can say that again,' said Muck, and Manchán blinked. Muck was the best pig in Ireland but even Muck couldn't talk. Not human talk anyway.

A pair of feet appeared under Manchán's nose. One of them had six toes. There was only one foot that Manchán knew with six toes on it.

'Pagan,' he said with a sigh. 'Thank Crom. Get me out of here.'

Pagan-of-the-Six-Toes was Manchán's pal, his best pal. Everything that Manchán wasn't, Pagan was, and then some – like with the sixth toe. And that included the bad stuff and the good stuff too. For example, Manchán could hit a sliotar farther than most men, but Pagan, who couldn't hit the ground if he fell on it, could run so fast he could belt after the sliotar with a good chance of catching it at the other end. And Pagan was clever. That was the only area in which he and Manchán were nearly exactly matched; though Pagan had better luck.

Pagan shoved Muck out of the way and reached down to grab Manchán's hands.

'On the count of three,' he said. '*One —*'

Manchán shouted, 'It's an emergency for Crom's sake, just pull!'

'*Three,*' said Pagan, and pulled.

Nothing happened. Manchán felt like his arms were about to pop their sockets, but didn't budge.

'Breathe out,' said Pagan. 'Make yourself thinner.'

Manchán breathed out and Pagan pulled again. He pulled and pulled and still nothing happened.

'Manchán's stuck,' said Méabh, suddenly appearing. 'I bet his tunic is caught in the wall! Hi, Pagan,' she added and wiggled her fingers at him.

Méabh liked Pagan, which made Pagan very uncomfortable. The last thing a peaceful person like him wanted was Méabh turning her attention on him.

'I heard Muck squealing,' said Méabh, 'and I knew something was going on. I'd say you

have about the space of five breaths before the parents come looking. Five, four, three …' Méabh started counting as well. But being Méabh she counted backwards to heighten the tension. 'Two, one!'

In the hut behind him, Manchán felt, rather than heard, the deerskin door being pushed to one side. A cold wind soughed over his backside, presenting, as it did, a tempting target sticking out of the wall for anybody who might be annoyed enough to give it a good kick.

'Manchán,' roared his father, and everybody heard him.

'Manchán,' screamed his mother, who had just joined her daughter at the corner of the hut.

'Told you,' remarked Méabh to Brother

Abstemius, who had just joined his sister to watch Manchán's disgrace.

'Pagan,' said Manchán desperately. 'PULL!!!'

Pagan pulled. With a sound like a foot being tugged from the Bog of Squelch, he yanked Manchán straight out of the hole. He hauled so hard that he tumbled backwards and Manchán continued on over his head and sprawled into the mud behind. His tunic stayed caught in the wall.

'Manchán,' shouted his mother, 'put some clothes on right now!'

But Manchán was already up and running. Naked or not, if he could make it to the coracle he still had a chance to escape the fate his parents were forcing on him. He ran and ran.

And Muck ran with him. Just a boy and his pig setting out into the great world beyond the river. Who knew what adventures would befall them? Maybe some day, somebody would even write those adventures down.

Behind him Brother Abstemius picked up the hurley stick that Manchán had abandoned and weighed it in one hand. From under his tunic he pro-  duced a turnip, a hard, round root about the size and shape of a baby's head. An ugly baby's head! Quick as a greyhound he took two steps forward and flipped the turnip into the air. There was a dull crack as the blade of the stick met its target and the whole family watched, including Manchán's father, now peering through the hole in the hut, while the turnip rose in an arc against the grey sky, then swiftly dropped and connected with the running boy below. It hit him right between the shoulder blades. Manchán stumbled and fell. A second later the noise of his shout floated back to his family on the breeze.

'Good shot, horse,' said Manchán's father, impressed, despite himself. He hadn't known that Brother Abstemius had an arm for hurling. He had thought him more the *reading* type.

'He's not hurt, is he? asked Manchán's mother.

'Hurt?' said Brother Abstemius, lifting just the one eyebrow this time. 'A punt from a turnip is no more serious than a good thump of a hurley stick,' he said.

Méabh frowned. 'Does that mean no?' she asked.

Manchán sat up and groaned. A few short beats of the heart ago he had been getting ready to call on Pagan and go off fishing, or maybe do a bit of hunting, but in any case just generally hang out and have a brilliant time. Now he was sitting in the mud beside a pig and a turnip, without any clothes on. How in the name of Crom had that happened? And why were those kinds of things always happening to *him*?

He looked back towards his traitorous family. Méabh was grinning from ear to ear and he could just see her doing a brain-polish on the story she would tell to everybody later on, making sure that the whole village had a giant laugh at him. And Daddy's face was red because his head appeared to have gotten stuck in the hole in the hut and serve him right. But most dangerous of all, Brother Abstemius was aiming a finger at him and crooking it like a hook to haul him in, and there was nothing he could do about it. *Caught is caught*, thought Manchán furiously, eyeing his hurley stick in the brother's other hand. Who knew how many other nasty, lumpy turnips the man had up his sleeve, and where in the name of Crom had he learned to hit a target like that, anyway?

'All right, all right, I'm coming,' shouted Manchán, standing up and feeling behind his back for the sore bit where he had been thumped out of the blue.

'Don't forget the turnip,' called his mother, across the field. 'Pick it up and bring it back with you. That's your dinner.'

Manchán looked at the turnip. It was a horrible thing, warty and leathery, like a shrunken head, and the coating of mud didn't make it any more beautiful. Manchán looked at Muck. When he wasn't messing around playing games, Muck was a well-trained pig and Manchán had put a lot of work into training him. Muck could be very obedient when he liked. Now Muck stared at the turnip and waited. At least somebody gets something out of all this, thought Manchán, and clicked twice with his tongue. Muck pounced on the turnip and started munching.

'Manchán,' shrieked his mother, but it was too late.

CHAPTER TWO

n which Manchán is forced by his Mother to get up early and do Chores on the Day of Rest. A brief Incursion to the Land of Dreams. A Boat Trip and an Introduction to the Lake Fairies. The Worm. A narrow Escape. Penance.

It was the Day of Rest, but Manchán's mother wasn't having any of it, not for him anyway. 'Get up, Manchán,' she snapped, and jabbed his foot with the bundle of twigs she used to sweep the floor of their hut. 'Get up,' she said again and, stepping across the room, she yanked back the deerskin door. An axe-shaped wedge of light split the room in two.

Manchán groaned and squashed his eyes shut tight behind his eyelids. He knew from experience that he had about the space of two breaths before he heard the swish of the twigs as his mother stepped up her efforts to encourage him

to leave his sheepskin bed. And once his mother had made up her mind to do something, there was little anyone could do to stop her, not even Ollmhór the village chieftain, who was seven feet tall and covered in scars from battle.

'Get up,' said his mother, in her this-is-your-last-chance tone of voice.

Manchán got up.

He opened his eyes and immediately his brain was scalded by the light from outside. Behind his eyelids, deep in the Land of Dreams, he had been riding a giant horse over a green meadow. Balancing on one foot, he had skillfully steered the galloping stallion with only the gentlest of pressure from his toes. Then his toes had prickled unpleasantly and that was where his mother had come in.

'I'm up,' he said. 'I'm up.'

And he was. The floor felt cold and damp under his feet. The sheepskin bed exhaled its warmth behind him.

'About time,' said his mother. 'The day is nearly over.' She thrust a sack of oats at him, and he grabbed hold. 'Now follow me,' she said. 'And no mucking about.'

Manchán followed.

Outside, the village was empty. It was the Day of Rest and everybody else was doing just that, resting. But everybody else wasn't in trouble, and everybody else (except Méabh) didn't have a mother like Manchán's, still annoyed, one week later, that her only son hadn't gone off monking with Brother Abstemius and bringing Honour to the Family. Instead, the exact opposite had occurred and 'Honour to the Family' had become a mocking phrase for every fool in the village to laugh at.

'Perhaps,' said Brother Abstemius before leaving, 'we should dwell on the matter a little while longer. I will pray for you, Manchán,' he added.

Manchán scowled in return.

'How will we ever live this down?' said Manchán's mother after her brother departed. Manchán's father just sighed.

In his wife's current mood, even the mildest expression of cautious disagreement could draw down thunder on his head to equal the blast that had split the great standing stone, lying since that time in two pieces just outside their village.

'Aye,' he agreed, 'it's terrible altogether, just terrible,' and affected a face so long he could have passed for a sheep in his woolly tunic.

But living it down was what they would have to do, or at least what Manchán would have to do on the family's behalf, and in the world according to his mother, that meant chores and more chores and, most especially, getting up early – and this in the era when getting up early really meant something! As part of his punishment, Manchán had been getting up early now for six days in a row, and that was a big part of the reason he had been so much looking forward to the Day of Rest. Instead he found himself standing in his bare feet in the mud outside their hut, shivering as the sun lifted over the trees, stirring with weak warmth the mist that oozed up from the ground and eddied through the village.

'See you later, Manchán,' called Méabh from inside the hut. 'Don't get sunburned.'

But Manchán ignored her. What was the point in saying anything when Méabh would just say something back and he would only have to answer that one too. And Méabh was hard to answer.

'Come on, Manchán,' said his mother, striking out towards the lake.

'Come on, Muck,' said Manchán, heaving the sack of oats onto one shoulder and heading off after his mother. And Muck said nothing,

just trotted happily after his Lord and Master. He didn't care one squeak about being up and about so early. Why would he, being a pig?

They walked quickly, or rather Manchán's mother walked quickly, as she always did, while Manchán struggled to keep up. The bag of oats dragged at his shoulder and twice he nearly slipped. If he knew where they were going, he thought, he might be able to suggest a shortcut, but his mother wasn't saying and maybe it was a surprise she was planning; an unpleasant surprise, of course, one clearly involving work. You didn't have to be a druid to work that one out.

They passed Bacmala's place. He was the beekeeper who lived just outside the village. The air around his hut was sweet and soft with somnolent buzzing. That was Bacmala snoring, buzzing away through his nose. But his bees were sleeping too, their wings still wet from the morning dew.

Everybody's sleeping, thought Manchán irritably, *except me*, though he didn't speak the thought out loud. He just kept on keeping up.

They left the village and followed the path to the right. The path sloped down through a rocky field, where it forked like the devil's tongue, one end snaking into the Tangled Forest, the other twisting towards a muddy patch with reeds where the family coracle was kept at the edge of the lake. This was the place that Manchán had been making for the week before, in his great break for freedom. He would have made it too, if it hadn't been for Brother Abstemius and that wretched turnip. Now he wondered if this was where his mother was leading him. But why? She hated boats. And fishing. On the other hand, she wasn't too fond of the forest either, full as it was of wolves and nettles. Maybe she was just going to tramp around the village in a circle, thought Manchán, to teach him some kind of weird lesson, and make him carry the bag of oats until he fainted. His mother swung towards the coracle.

Now the path turned boggy, but at least it was a path, sort of. Some years before, in a spasm of home-improvements, Manchán's father had banged a series of wooden pegs into the ground, then laid down rush and logs between them, building a rough if slippery path to the lake.

'Like the Romans,' he said proudly when he finished, a tribe of road-builders he had heard of from the other side of the world, who were now long gone but whose roads outlived them.

Unlike your path, thought Manchán, remembering the comment and feeling down between the mud with his toes, struggling to find the remnants of his father's work. But at least the sack seemed easier to carry and the coracle was just about a hop, a step and a lep away.

'Nearly there, Muck,' said Manchán, shifting the sack to his other shoulder, while behind him his pig squeaked and snuffled and snorted. Muck liked walking in the mud.

His mother arrived at the coracle. She bent over and untied the leather line, then turned as Manchán came up beside her.

'Now,' she began, and stopped. 'Oh, for Crom's sake,' she said crossly.

Manchán said, 'What?'

In the same second he felt something brushing against his leg.

He looked down to see a small trickle of oats pouring out of the sack and falling like a miniature snow storm to the ground. No wonder the sack felt lighter. And at his feet, Muck snuffled and snorted the oats in through his snout.

'Muck,' groaned his master, and Muck stopped eating. Manchán put the sack on the ground and twisted it shut.

'It wasn't my fault,' said Manchán.

'It never is,' said his mother. She grabbed the coracle to hold it steady. 'Get in,' she said.

Manchán got in. Muck followed.

'Now,' said his mother, 'you are the boy to

take the coracle without permission. But this time you have my permission. Take these oats to Brother Abstemius and tell him they are a gift to replace the turnip you fed to your pig. With our apologies. Especially yours.'

With a quick movement, she tossed the leather line to Manchán, landing it across his chest and face. Manchán folded his arms. 'No,' he said, 'I won't.'

'Yes,' said his mother, 'you will.' And she gave the coracle a hard shove to send it out beyond the reeds.

'I will not,' said Manchán, keeping his balance and standing up straight in the boat. The coracle was round and deep, like a barrel with a curved bottom, and Manchán was light. When he stood, his waist came up to the tarred rim. (When his father sat in the coracle, the rim of the boat came up to his armpits and it looked like he was sitting in a hole in the water.) And Muck, sitting at Manchán's feet, had no view at all, apart from up.

The coracle moved suddenly again, and now Manchán grabbed at the sides to stay upright. His mother was shoving it with the oar, pushing it further out. The coracle turned slightly as it scraped through the reeds, and a duck that had been hiding nearby clattered away over the still surface of the lake.

Manchán said angrily, 'I know what you're up to. You just want me to go to the monastery and then change my mind. But I won't.'

'Only a fool won't change his mind,' said his mother, not bothering to deny the accusation. She stepped out into the shallows to give the coracle another push.

Manchán said, 'Well, why won't *you* change *yours?*' Then he fell as the coracle tipped violently back and forth, before sliding out silently beyond the reeds.

Manchán landed on the oats beside Muck. Above his head the low sky spun slowly. He sat up and glared back towards the shore. Now only the top of his head and his eyes were showing, staring over the rim like an angry frog.

Returning to the shore, his mother jammed the thin end of the oar hard with one fist into the mud, like a spear. Then she rammed the other fist into her side and leaning forward, shouted, 'Manchán, you can either row across the lake and take those oats to my brother and have a look at the monastery while you're at it, then be home in time for dinner. Or you can walk around the lake carrying the oats and do the same and be back tomorrow instead. That's your choice. Now make up your mind.'

Then, without waiting for him to make up his mind, she turned and walked quickly back up the path until she vanished from view behind the rocks and the bushes. *That is so unfair,* thought Manchán, and Muck nodded. Or it seemed to Manchán that he nodded, though maybe it was just the movement of the boat. Then Manchán shouted, 'Wait … the oar!' But his mother was gone.

The lake was deep and cold. At least in the middle it was. At its edges it was shallow and cold. The lake was served by a thin, wriggling river that broadened out at one end where it flowed on towards the sea. For this reason it was called the Lake of the Worm. Or maybe it was called that because of the giant worm-like crea-

ture that coursed through its depths, eating the fish and whatever else it took a fancy to. This was according to Pagan's grandfather, Fionn-of-the-Question, who knew about such things.

When the weather was rough, the lake's surface was chopped by toothy waves, and made for bad fishing. On foggy days the surface was flat, like syrup, and if you listened carefully you might hear the voices of the lake fairies, calling you to dive down into their watery kingdom, from which you would never return.

'Two very good reasons never to learn to swim,' Manchán's father had said, 'the fairies and the Worm, so even if you are tempted by the wicked creatures, you won't be able to act on the temptation, and ignorance will keep you safe.'

Méabh said, 'But isn't the point of their singing to lure you into the water to drown, so if you could swim, then you might actually escape them?'

Her father scratched his head.

'And what happens if you fall out of the coracle while fishing?' asked Méabh. 'You could drown then, with or without the lake fairies? So wouldn't it be better, in that case, to know how to swim?'

Her father brightened. He was back on territory that he understood. 'You can't fall out of a coracle,' he said. 'It's too round!'

Méabh laughed shortly. 'I bet Manchán could,' she said.

Now Manchán sat in the coracle without any oar and remembered this conversation. He wondered if his father was right, though the last thing he wanted to do was put it to the test. The fact was, he couldn't swim, and already the coracle had drifted far enough out onto the

lake for the water to be deeper than Manchán could stand up in.

And what about Muck? What would Muck do if he fell in? According to Pagan, this wouldn't be a problem, as all animals could swim if they had to, cows, goats, pigs, even hedgehogs. Assuming, of course, the Worm didn't come shooting up out of the depths and swallow them in one mighty gulp.

'We're in it now Muck,' said Manchán gloomily, and he wasn't talking about the boat either.

The coracle drifted on. Manchán put his nose over the side and peered down at the fish below. *How easy they have it*, he thought, *except for the giant Worm, of course, and my father too – who isn't a bad fisherman, and who nearly always comes home with his basket full. But other than that, how easy is their life!*

The fish flickered lazily through the weeds and didn't even seem to notice the coracle over their heads.

Strange, thought Manchán. *We would surely notice if a ship appeared above us in the air.* But maybe it was something to do with the nature of water. Or perhaps fish couldn't see up, just down.

He gazed back towards the shore. The oar was still there, like somebody thin watching him drift slowly away. Manchán shook his head. The oar was definitely his mother's fault, but he knew that when he mentioned it later, she would find some way to twist it into his doing.

'Well, why didn't you shout after me?' she would ask.

'I did,' Manchán would say, 'but you didn't hear me.'

'Well, why didn't you shout louder?' she would reply.

'Because I had already shouted as loud as I could,' Manchán would answer.

'So what did you do all day?' she would ask next.

'I sat in the boat and drifted.'

'So you never got to the monastery?'

'How could I, without an oar to row with?'

In his head, Manchán always won the argument, though rarely in real life. Now he sat down on the oat-sack in the boat, leaning against the side, with Muck warm at his feet. The boat drifted while the sun tried to burn away the mist and the lake water lapped against the leather and lulled him slowly to sleep. Maybe he would end up getting his Day of Rest after all. Maybe this was it. Slowly, slowly, he descended into the Land of Dreams, and his boat drifted with him.

Manchán woke with a start. That was the thing about the Land of Dreams. Mostly it was a pleasant visit, like with the horse this morning, but sometimes it was so horrible, you were desperate to leave. Now was one of the horrible times. In the Land of Dreams he had been standing in a pot full of porridge and bacon while a devil stirred it with an oar and farted loudly onto the flames to make the fire roar. The devil looked like Brother Abstemius and sang while he stirred. It was the singing that woke him.

Manchán stood up on the bag of oats. The bag seemed floppier than it had been and Muck looked fatter. But now was not the time

to worry about that. He peered out over the rim of the coracle and tried to see where the singing was coming from. But the world was still misty and the weak sun a disc of light that was barely visible. He cupped his hands behind his ears and listened hard. There it was again. A kind of high-pitched keening, like a wolf with stomach cramps, or worse.

The song twisted and turned. It sounded like the singer was having a hard time keeping up with the tune. Slowly, Manchán started to make out individual words, only they were words that he couldn't understand. Alarmed, he ducked back down inside the coracle.

'It's the lake fairies,' he whispered to Muck, 'trying to lure us to our doom.' Then he poked his nose up over the rim again.

The singing grew louder. That meant the fairies were coming towards him. Or maybe it meant that he was drifting in their direction, only without an oar there was nothing he could do to prevent it. He jammed his fingers into his ear holes but the sound leaked in like smoke through a tightly woven basket. He tried folding his ears over and pressing them shut with the palms of his hands, but that was so painful he stopped almost immediately. The song wound on. Whichever fairy was singing had a horrible voice, though as yet Manchán didn't feel one bit tempted to throw himself into the lake. Probably that was coming, thought Manchán gloomily. Probably the fairy only needed to be a little closer for the spell to work. Then he perked up. If that was the case, then maybe he still had a chance to get away. Manchán looked at his hands. 'You can't fall out of a coracle,' he said to Muck, then he leaned forward hard over the side and started paddling.

The song kept on. Manchán paddled as fast as he could. In the bottom of the coracle Muck squealed loudly as water splashed down on his back.

'Hush, Muck,' hissed Manchán, trying to splash less and paddle more. The coracle started turning in a slow, sweeping circle. Manchán thrashed on like a big-bottomed beetle, fallen into the water and waving its feelers feebly and getting nowhere at all. He tried paddling in the other direction and the coracle turned slowly that way now, but still only turned. At the bottom of the boat Muck squealed and kept on squealing. That was nearly as bad as the stupid song.

'Muck,' said Manchán, 'for the love of Crom, stop squealing.'

But Muck didn't listen. Something must be wrong. Manchán stopped paddling and looked. The bottom of the coracle had at least the width of two fists of water in it and the sack of oats was swollen tight and ready to burst.

'Oh, porridge,' said Manchán and groaned. Maybe you couldn't fall out of a coracle, but you could certainly fill one with water and sink it, and that would end up being pretty much the same thing. He bent down and cupped the water with his hands, scooping it back out into the lake. And as he scooped, something strange and long slid in and out of view up ahead, a thin thing, a hunched thing, glimpsed and gone again as the mist thickened around it.

Manchán's hair stood up like grass and he crouched down quickly in the boat, trying not to breathe or be heard breathing.

'It's a fairy boat, Muck,' he whispered, 'out hunting for us. Whatever plan we come up with, it had better be a quick one.' And Muck nodded, or maybe it was just the coracle rocking. Which-ever it was, coming up with a plan was more Manchán's job than his, he being a pig and all.

But Manchán's plan-store was empty. The problem was, he had almost nothing to work with. He thought about Pagan. Sometimes when Manchán needed an idea, he asked himself what Pagan would do, though this time nothing entered his brain. Next he consulted Méabh, but in his head he could only hear her laughing at his predicament, and that wasn't helpful at all. He looked around the boat. He had a pig and some oats, a leather line and himself. That was it. He thought of Pagan again and wished fervently that he was there. Then a finger snapped somewhere deep in his mind, something that Pagan said, something about animals. And Manchán remembered.

'Come here, Muck,' he said, and he grabbed his pig and tied the leather line tight round his back. He couldn't tie it around his neck because Muck didn't have a neck, so his back would have to do. Then he tied the other end to a rib inside the coracle. He picked Muck up.

'I'm sorry, Muck,' he said, 'but the line is good and strong and the worst that will happen is that you'll get a bath.'

Then he threw Muck over the side. There

was a squeal, and a splash, and silence.

The singing stopped. The line ran out. Manchán stared at the spreading circle where Muck had gone.

'Is somebody there?' said a voice from the mist, while Manchán gripped the rim and didn't answer. He wasn't stupid. He wasn't about to give away his position. Let the fairies come and find him if they could.

The line snapped tight. The coracle tilted, then rocked as the line went loose.

'Muck,' said Manchán, panicking, grabbing the line and ready to haul his pig back on board.

Then the water buckled up beyond, as a sudden surge of snout broke the surface and Muck appeared, nose-holes thrusting in the air, all four legs working, swimming like a fat dark frog with pink ears. Pagan was right after all.

The line snapped tight and the coracle began moving forward.

'Go on, you mighty pig,' screamed Manchán, then clamped a hand over his mouth as an answering shout came out of the mist behind him.

'Reveal yourself,' commanded the voice loudly.

'Go on, Muck,' hissed Manchán. 'Swim for your life.' *And mine too*, he thought, but didn't say.

Pulled by his pig, he moved off into the mist where he planned to hide and leave the horrible singing far behind him.

The mist turned to fog. Muck splashed bravely on. The fog deadened all sound like a blanket. Of all the stupid days, thought Manchán, to send him across the lake, this was certainly the stupidest, and that would be the first thing he pointed out to his mother when he saw her again. If he saw her again!

The next thing would be to organise a boat race with Pagan and maybe some of the others on the hurling team. They could use different animals and even change the design of the

coracle to make it go faster, or to somehow steer it a bit. He looked at Muck. It seemed like he was swimming to the right.

'Go straight, Muck,' he hissed, tugging on the line, 'straight!'

Glancing behind him, he could see that Muck was pulling him in a circle. That wasn't good at all, as the last place he wanted to end up was the place they had just left. He tugged harder on the line. Maybe he had tied it crooked and that was the problem. He pulled again and the knot slipped slightly but held. 'Oh, Crom,' said Manchán and immediately stopped pulling. The last thing he needed was for Muck to go swimming off into the mist without him.

'Muck,' he hissed, then ducked down quickly out of view as the silhouette of the fairy boat appeared up ahead, this time no further away than the hop of a skimmed stone. He peeped over the rim and stared at the fairies. There were three of them, backs turned, all completely silent, listening out for him no doubt. For a second the fog thinned and he caught a proper

glimpse of the middle one, ugly and bent, with
hair like thistle furze and a long finger of a nose
pointing this way and that. Two other fairies sat
in the boat with him, one tall, one squat like a
toad, with ears like oyster shells. That was the
way of fairies, thought Manchán, they could be
beautiful as apples or ugly as mould. Just like
people. Then the fog closed its hand again and
the fairy boat was gone. *We're going to make it,*
thought Manchán in relief. They nearly did too.

One moment it was quiet, Muck swimming
strongly, the leather line between him and the
boat twanging softly, snapping fat droplets onto
the lake's surface. A second later there was a great

erupting splash and a piercing squeal as Muck turned and thrashed in the water. Manchán could see that something had wrapped itself around him and was trying to pull him under. He was fighting it with all his piggy might.

The Worm, thought Manchán, cursing his own forgetfulness and standing straight up in the coracle, all thoughts of fairies forgotten. How could he have been so stupid! A pig thrown into the water on the end of a line was perfect bait for the Worm, and the Worm had taken it.

'Muck,' shouted Manchán, 'hang on!' And he hauled hard on the line.

But Muck didn't budge. Instead the coracle skimmed forward as Manchán pulled. Now he could see poor Muck, roiling under the lake's surface, the horrible grey coils of the Worm winding around him, dragging him down.

'I'm coming, Muck,' shouted Manchán, and he was. He tugged the line tight and leaned forward, sticking out a hand to grab his best pig. In that second the knot slipped, and Manchán fell out of the coracle. The Worm wrapped itself around him.

So this is how it ends, thought Manchán bitterly, *drowned by the stupid Worm*. Méabh would have a good laugh at that – later on anyway, when she had gotten over being sad and missing him. And his mother would feel bad too, for a long time hopefully.

The Worm grabbed Manchán's neck and leg.

'Aaagh!' shouted Manchán, his lungs filling up with lake water.

Then the Worm grabbed his hair and pulled. *What kind of a worm has hands?* thought Manchán, coughing as his head came up out of the lake and his legs scraped over something rough and hard. The coils fell away and he landed, choking, on his back. Something poked him in the belly and he started wheezing.

He wheezed and coughed until he felt like he could cough no more but at least when it was done he found that he could breathe again.

'Muck,' he gasped. 'Is Muck all right?'

A voice he knew said, 'If you are referring to your pig, he's fine.'

Manchán opened his eyes. The three fairies were staring at him, one uglier than the next, but they weren't fairies at all. At least the middle one definitely wasn't.

'Can't a monk enjoy his Day of Rest, and a bit of morning song and fishing without some-body coming along and wrecking his nets?' growled Brother Abstemius.

Nets, thought Manchán, *not the Worm!* But all he said was, 'It wasn't my fault.'

'Of course not,' said Brother Abstemius. 'It must have been mine.'

Manchán said nothing.

'Brother Hideus,' continued Brother Abstemius to the monk in the currach beside him, the one with the long nose. 'This is my sister's son, Manchán, the one I am praying about.' Brother

Hideus nodded briskly, like a woodpecker with hiccups, and stayed silent.

'Brother Cook,' said Brother Abstemius to the monk on his right, 'what are we having for dinner tonight?'

Brother Cook considered the question. He was a fat, squat man without a pick of jolly in him.

'Turnips,' he said at last, 'and maybe fish.'

Manchán groaned out loud. He knew what

was coming next. Brother Abstemius smiled at his nephew. 'Let's talk about your penance,' he said.

CHAPTER THREE

n which Manchán and Pagan are sent to gather Berries and Manchán admires the View while Pagan works. A Fairy Circle and a great Fight. The lost Ball and a long Walk Home. Tricked!

t was late afternoon and Manchán and Pagan-of-the-Six-Toes were out picking berries. A whole fortnight had passed since the fishing incident and Manchán was beginning to hope that his uncle had changed his mind about taking him to the monastery. He would have prayed if he thought it would help, but that might encourage his mother, so mostly he tried just not thinking about it. Manchán was good at not thinking about stuff, unless it was nice stuff, of course, like fishing, or being out in the sun picking berries or, better still, eating them.

For Manchán loved berries. He especially liked berries with cream and he loved the way the black ones turned the thick cream purple when he stirred it with his fingers. 'Manchán,' Méabh would say, 'eat with your spoon,' but Manchán would ignore her. First of all she wasn't his mother. Second of all, fingers were more fun than spoons. Now he rubbed his fingers hard against his tunic. For some reason they were completely sticky at the moment.

Beside him Pagan was picking busily. He had a reed basket on his arm and it was nearly half full already. He had rowan berries and blueberries and blackberries, great handfuls of each kind, all laid down carefully on leaves to stop them turning mushy. Manchán's own basket was emptier; much emptier. He had one blueberry, two blackberries and three rowan berries. At least he thought they were rowan berries until Pagan saw them.

'You can't eat those,' he said, when Manchán joined him.

'Why not?' said Manchán.

'Because you'll die,' said Pagan.

Well, that was a good reason, Manchán supposed.

'I thought they were rowan berries,' he said.

Pagan shook his head. 'Those are yew berries,' he said. 'Rowan berries aren't pale red, like that. And rowan berries come in bunches, like frogspawn, not singly. And when you squash them, rowan berries aren't sticky.'

Manchán looked at his fingers. They were practically glued together.

'Don't lick them,' said Pagan. 'Not unless you want to throw up, and if you do, then point in the other direction, please.'

'You're worse than Méabh for nagging,' said Manchán indignantly. 'Of course I'm not going to lick them.'

'Thank you, Pagan,' said Pagan, 'for just saving my life.' 'You're welcome, Manchán,' he said, answering himself, then went back to picking.

Pagan was the best picker in the village. *He should have been called Pagan-of-the-Six-Fingers*, thought Manchán, he was that speedy. And Manchán was the worst, except for Brian the Blind, for obvious reasons. But Manchán didn't like picking berries, only eating them. Picking them was a pain and nearly as bad as penance in his opinion.

He tossed his sliotar onto his hurley stick and bounced it twice. Then he took aim at a round rock nearby surrounded by a ring of mushrooms, and let fly. *Whack! Score!* The sliotar bounced hard off the rock and flew back towards his head. He blocked it with his stick and caught it. Then he jumped over the mushrooms, hopped up onto the rock and sat down. *One–nil to Manchán. Against a rock!* He placed his hurley stick down beside him with the blade on top of the sliotar to keep it from rolling away. Then he tossed the three poisonous berries out of the basket onto the grass, where Muck sat just outside the circle and

ignored them completely. Muck was a clever
pig, with good instincts. Poisonous berries and
fairy rings were two things best avoided.

Manchán looked around him. It was a fine
bright day and he was sitting high up on the hill,

a good long walk from the village. The Lake of the Worm was a shining puddle of silver poured into the valley below, and the river flowing through it seemed to wriggle like a living thing. In the middle of the lake was Hag island and on

the other side rose the monastery with its great stone church and the small beehive huts where the monks lived. Further away was the coast and the wild-waved sea, a glimpse of churning white through a split in the far-off hills.

Manchán shivered. That had been a narrow escape the week before, he thought, thinking of Brother Abstemius and the Worm, although it hadn't actually turned out to be the Worm after all. What would be the worse fate, he wondered, to be captured by the fairies or eaten by the Worm? Both were equally bad. And what about the monking? Also bad, but possibly he would pick that if he had to. Anyway, Brother Abstemius was still praying about him. *Let him pray*, thought Manchán, *for as long as he wants.*

He glanced back towards Pagan, picking away like a blackbird, his hurley stick propped against the bush nearby. If Manchán had had his own stick with him in the coracle that day, he could have used it to fight the Worm. Or better still, as an oar, or a rudder at least, with Muck to pull. He pictured this in his mind and decided to try it out at some later date and see what happened, once he was able to persuade Muck to go anywhere near the lake again.

Manchán lay back on the rock. The sky over his head was blue and the air vibrated with the bright lovely singing of the larks. *Why can birds sing*, thought Manchán, *and pigs can't?* He had once tried to teach Muck to sing but it hadn't worked. And why could some people sing while others couldn't? His father was a great singer and Manchán himself wasn't bad, but Méabh and his mother had voices that would peel the bark from a tree. Nobody ever asked them for a song, that was certain. On the other hand, there were lots of other things they were good at instead, like criticising.

Manchán stood up and stretched. That last thought had punctured his relaxed mood and provoked him into action. Since the lake episode his mother had eased up on him a bit, but she still hadn't given up on her plan to send him off monking, so it certainly wouldn't do to go back to the village empty-handed.

'All right, Muck,' he said, 'it's time to get to work.'

He looked up and down the briar patch. Further along Pagan had already filled one basket and was starting on a second. He was concentrating on the blackberries now, his purple-stained fingers moving in a blur over the bush. Pagan had perfected a technique for picking with both hands, something nobody else could do. He seemed to know, just by looking, which berries were good and which were rotten. Manchán, on the other hand, had to pick each berry, then check the stem to see if it was rotten or not. More often than not he'd find a maggot in it, waving its little head at him. (Or was it its bottom? It was hard to tell with maggots.) Then Manchán would toss it over his shoulder so Muck would eat it, and the whole lengthy process would start again.

Manchán sighed. Why couldn't they be out picking mushrooms instead? Mushrooms were bigger, and they didn't have any thorns either. Plus they couldn't kill you, like berries could. Well, that bit wasn't true. But as long as you knew what kind to pick, you were all right. He looked at the ones growing in the ring around his rock. Were they edible? They certainly looked edible. But you had to be sure, to be sure.

Manchán kicked his hurley stick into his hand and jumped from the rock. He belted the sliotar into one of the larger mushrooms, breaking the circle and knocking the cap from the stem. Upside down, the cap was a greeny colour and frilled with yellow gills. In the middle, where the stem had broken off, the centre was turning blue. Manchán picked up the cap and sniffed it. It smelt like earth and old leaves, and something else besides, something standing just out of sight at the edge of his mind.

'Here, Muck,' he said, holding the cap out towards him, but Muck, still sitting just outside the circle, kept his mouth closed tightly and didn't even sniff and it seemed to Manchán that he might have shaken his head if he could.

'Pagan,' shouted Manchán then and, tossing the mushroom into the air, he whirled his hurley stick expertly in a quick, smooth arc. 'Look!'

As Pagan looked (still picking, the show-off) the blade hit the mushroom and exploded it into a thousand soft bits. 'Two–nil to Manchán,' shouted Manchán, as Muck stood up and stepped away a bit, then sat back down again.

Pagan snorted loudly. 'Against a mushroom,' he said. Then he said, 'Listen, Manchán, if you don't start picking soon it will be dark and we'll have to be going back and I swear to Crom I won't be giving you any of my berries either, no matter what you say!'

'All right, all right,' shouted Manchán. 'Crom almighty!'

He swung his hurley stick again and whacked another three of the mushrooms, *whack, thwack, smack*, then stamped a couple into the ground for fun, before hopping out of the circle and walking reluctantly towards the blackberry bush, kicking his basket in front of him. Muck stayed where he was.

The bush was brambly and brown and bare and most of the berries at eye-level were gone.

'For Crom's sake, Pagan,' said Manchán indignantly, 'how am I supposed to pick anything when you've gone and stripped the bush to begin with? Some friend you are!'

He scowled and stretched out his hand for the remaining berries. And just then, something stung him on the back of his neck.

'Ow,' said Manchán, and felt with his hand. His fingers came away red and for a second he thought that he was bleeding. But there were bits in the red and he saw that it was a ripe blackberry that had hit him, the size of a bumblebee. 'Hey,' he shouted at Pagan, who had his back turned, pretending!

Manchán frowned. He bent over and pulled a berry from the bush, then fired it in Pagan's direction. *Missed, blast it!* And Pagan didn't even seem to notice. *Hmmph*, thought Manchán, then went back to picking, until another berry struck.

'OW,' said Manchán, louder this time, and rubbed the second red splotch on his neck. Who would have thought that blackberries could be so painful?

He straightened up and shook his fist at Pagan. 'I'm warning you,' he said.

'About what?' said Pagan, looking genuinely puzzled.

'You know what,' said Manchán, annoyed, looking around for a nice fat blackberry to return fire. That last one was probably too small; he needed one with a bit of weight in it.

There, he spotted one, dangling right under his nose, with its fat juicy twin beside it. Two huge blackberries, each the size of his thumb. That was odd. How in the name of Crom could he have missed seeing them to begin with? He picked the berries and checked their stems.

'How'ye maggot,' he said with a grin. Nice and ripe – and inhabited! He aimed carefully and threw hard.

'Ow,' said Pagan, and groped the back of his neck.

'Ha,' said Manchán, 'how do you like that?'

Then, as Pagan turned around, he threw the other one, even harder, and scored again!

'HEY,' said Pagan, looking down at the red splat on his tunic. 'That was my clean shirt.'

'Not any more,' said Manchán and laughed. 'Serves you right,' he added, 'and now we're quits.'

'Quits,' said Pagan loudly, 'for what?' And he glared at Manchán.

'For attacking me when my back was turned,' said Manchán. 'For no reason at all,' he added piously.

'*I* attacked *you*?' said Pagan angrily, and he raised two berry-laden fists. 'Are you mad?'

'Not once, but twice,' shouted Manchán, glancing quickly at the bush beside him. Sud-

ddenly, just within reach were some of the fattest, ripest blackberries he had ever seen, enough to fill two baskets – or to pound Pagan so hard he'd look like he'd been dipped headfirst in the Bog of Squelch. He stretched out a hand.

With one arm held up to shield his face, Manchán picked hard and returned fire with the other. And every time he reached for the bush it seemed like a blackberry simply sprouted like magic under his fingers. He picked and threw and picked and threw, and Pagan, not to be outdone, redoubled his efforts so that anybody watching from afar would have thought that the two small boys were battling against a swarm of bees. The fighting only stopped when Manchán misgrabbed and his hand closed unluckily on a briar.

'Aaaghh,' he shouted, as the thorns bit into his fingers, then twisted around his tunic, and his arm was caught.

'Ha ha,' roared Pagan, 'I've got you now!' Caught up in the battle and picking up his full basket of berries, he advanced quickly on his enemy.

'Truce,' shouted Manchán, tugging at his tunic, but Pagan kept coming.

'You started it,' Pagan shouted, 'and I'm ending it,' and he dumped his basket of berries right onto Manchán's head, then fell on top of him, mushing them into his hair and face as hard as he could.

Manchán's tunic ripped under Pagan's weight and he collapsed to the ground, and as he fell he glimpsed a pair of merry eyes watching him from rabbit-level in the brambles. Only it wasn't a rabbit. Then, with a blink, they were gone.

'Stop,' he shouted weakly to Pagan, 'stop!'

'Do you submit?' roared Pagan.

'I submit,' wheezed Manchán.

'Yeearrrrghhh,' bellowed Pagan in triumph, letting Manchán go. Then, falling back on  the grass, he laughed and laughed and laughed some more. And because it was so funny and because they were blackened with berries and stickled with briars, and because his tunic was torn and his mother would kill him and there was nothing he could do about it anyway, Manchán joined in too, and laughed and laughed and laughed as hard. And a little farther away, watching the laughing boys, Muck did in fact shake his head – though, as nobody saw him, who knows? Maybe it was just a trick of the light and the lengthening shadows and the evening coming down around them.

'I'm for it now,' said Manchán, when he finally stopped laughing. His hair stuck out at all angles and his hands and face and tunic looked like he had been rolling in blackberries, which was pretty close to the truth when you think about it. 'My mother is going to kill me,' he added, and Pagan nodded as this was pretty close to the truth as well. Pagan himself didn't look much better, only it didn't matter as much to him, as his grandfather never cared about stuff like that anyhow.

They sat on the hill and looked down over the Lake of the Worm. The evening light had turned the silver to rose which meant it was time for them to start heading home again. A small wind got up and blew a thin tune like laughter through the brambles behind them. Pagan picked up his battered basket and shrugged.

'Maybe we'll find a few berries on the way to placate your parents,' he said. 'I'll even give you any I find,' he added generously, knowing Manchán was in way more trouble than he was, a thing that was not seldom, but wasn't that what friends did for each other? 'Come on,' he said, standing up. 'Let's go.'

Manchán nodded and reached for his hurley stick. Then he looked around for his sliotar.

Had it rolled into the brambles, maybe? He got down on his hands and knees and checked. Behind the briars he saw a curve of white, and something else – those eyes again, just behind the ball, staring mischievously back at him.

'There's a rabbit in here,' he said to Pagan. 'At least, I *think* it's a rabbit.' But as he spoke, the eyes closed and vanished.

Lucky for you, rabbit, thought Manchán, poking into the brambles and groping after the sliotar with his stick. It must have taken a fierce kick in the heat of battle, he thought, to send it all the way in there. Then he noticed a green briar twisting off and up out of the heart of the bush. How had he not seen that before? It was as thick as his wrist and laden with berries, enough to fill six baskets. He plucked one with

his fingers and examined it. The stem was pale white and maggot-free.

'Crom's socks, Pagan,' said Manchán, 'but we are the boys with luck.' He tossed the berry to Muck, who ignored it completely. Then Manchán picked another and popped it in his own mouth instead. It tasted even better than it looked. A few quick handfuls of these and they'd be on their way home as heroes. He could come back and fetch his sliotar some other time.

The light was going and Bacmala's bees were returning to their hives when Bacmala got the

fright of his life at the approach of two lumpy devils emerging blackly from the fires of the setting sun. Then he heard Manchán singing and relaxed. 'Is it yourself Manchán?' he said, saluting the boys as they passed him by, baskets balanced on their heads. He wondered why they looked so filthy but, knowing Manchán, there would certainly be a reason, if not necessarily a good one. He wondered what was in the baskets they were carrying. They had a heavy, tasty look about them.

They came to the great standing stone marking the edge of their village, blasted back in the day by the storm and lying since then in two pieces.

'See you tomorrow, Manchán,' said Pagan, taking the path that led to the hut where he and his grandfather lived.

'See you tomorrow, Pagan,' replied Manchán, dropping the basket to one shoulder and squeezing through the split in the stone for luck – not that he would need it, he thought, for after all, wasn't he coming home with hands and basket full? 'Come on, Muck,' he said, and Muck squeezed through the stone and followed him.

Like Bacmala's hives, the village itself was settling down for the night, the house-fires warm and the people gathering and quietly active. The sun had dwindled to a thin copper wire on the brow of the hill and the sweet blue scent of turf smoke hung in the air. In the distance, somebody was playing a tune. Manchán stopped and listened. He knew all the tunes of the village but this was a new one to him. It was fine and dancing-light and sounded almost like laughter, the way some said fairy music was supposed to sound. He wondered whose hut it was coming from, but the tune drifted like the turf smoke and he couldn't tell. He listened, trying to fix it in his mind, until a voice called his name, and the tune was gone.

'Manchán,' said his father, coming up the path towards him. 'Are you deaf?'

'No,' said Manchán. 'Why?'

'Because I was calling you and you were standing here with your mouth open like you were half-cracked,' said his father, 'not answering me.'

Manchán looked around. The sun was gone and it was suddenly cold. What he needed most now was a fire and a blanket and something to eat.

'Come on,' said his father. 'Come home and get cleaned up quick, before your mother sees you.'

'Where is she?' asked Manchán, and his father jerked his head towards the other end of the village.

'She went looking for you,' he said. 'She was starting to think a wolf had eaten you up. Crom help him if he had,' he added.

They walked quickly towards the hut. Outside a small fire was burning and Méabh was sitting grinding oats with a quern. Manchán groaned internally. If his mother was gone then that meant Méabh would be making the evening meal, and Méabh was a miserable cook. 'You'll never get a husband if you don't learn how to cook,' said their mother from time to time, and Méabh always answered, 'I know.'

She looked up now as Manchán approached. 'I knew a wolf didn't get you,' she said. 'Why would he, when a sheep tastes better any day?' But then she smiled, and maybe she was pleased that he hadn't been eaten alive after all. She pushed a pot of water towards him. 'Here,' she said. 'It's warm.'

Manchán stripped off his tunic and squatted down beside his sister. He dipped his hands into the water and rubbed them on his face.

'Why are you so dirty?' asked Méabh. 'What were you up to?'

'Picking blackberries with Pagan,' said Manchán, scraping the bits out of his hair.

'Were you picking them with your head?' asked Méabh, and Manchán said, 'Ha ha.'

Then he said, 'You should see the state of Pagan, though,' and grinned. What a fine fight they'd had! Who would have thought that berry picking could be so much fun?

'Manchán,' said a voice behind him, 'why were you out so late and what

exactly do you have to grin about?' His mother stepped into the firelight.

Manchán blew out his cheeks and made his face look serious. 'I was just remembering all the blackberries I picked,' he sort-of-lied. 'And I was thinking about how nice and juicy they are.'

'You were picking berries in the dark?' said his mother unreasonably.

'It wasn't dark when he left,' said Méabh, amazingly taking Manchán's side for a change. But maybe she had her eye on a fill from the basket later on. Méabh loved berries. She looked at Manchán and gave him a sly wink.

'Have you finished grinding those oats yet?' asked Manchán's mother sharply.

'I have,' said Méabh.

'You haven't,' said her mother, 'not unless it's horses you're feeding. Now get back to work.' Méabh started turning the quern again.

'Pet,' said Daddy, 'Méabh is right. It's true that Manchán was gone for a long time, and it's also true that he did come back a little late, but picking is hard work and it was a heavy load he was carrying and maybe we shouldn't be too hard on the boy. And look what I have,' he added, shooting his last arrow. From behind his back he produced a small clay jug with a lid on it. 'Fine fresh cream,' he said, 'just waiting to embrace most sweetly a bowl of blackberries.

Now, what do you say?'

Manchán waited, though he could see from the look on his mother's face that his father had won. The cream had done the trick. His mother liked blackberries as much as Méabh did, if not even more, but blackberries and cream she adored.

'Go on, then,' she said, and squatted down beside him. 'Show us what you have.'

Manchán pulled the basket towards him. He had covered the berries with leaves to stop them bouncing out while he jogged home. He cleared his throat. 'It was a fine autumn morning when Pagan and I set out,' he began, but his mother interrupted him.

'Just show us,' she said. 'You can tell us the story later.'

Manchán nodded. That meant he wouldn't have to tell any story afterwards, which suited him just fine. He reached into the basket and grabbed a handful of the leaves. Then he lifted them up with a flourish.

The basket was full of acorns, dry and old and hard.

'Huh?' said Manchán, startled, and dug his hands deep into the rustling heap.

And somewhere in the distance, a tune was played, fine and dancing-light, with a sound like laughter.

CHAPTER FOUR

n which Manchán and his Father fix the Roof of their Hut while a fierce Gale rages. An even fiercer Gael and his mighty Ram. Manchán takes on the Ram while his Mother takes on the Chieftain. A swift Gallop to the Bog of Squelch. Some Betting, then a giant Leap and a Jig.

It was a hard, wild day and the clouds were tumbling inland from the coast. They scattered through the sky, high over the village, where Manchán was helping his father fasten the thatch to the roof of their hut with the help of an old fishing net.

'Pull,' shouted Manchán's father at Manchán, who had grabbed one side of the net and was hanging from it, feet dangling over the ground.

'I *am* pulling,' shouted Manchán, but the wind whipped his voice away to nothing. The thatch lifted like a hat and a gale tore into the hut like a giant hand stirring everything inside around and sending it flying, including Manchán's big sister

Méabh, sitting peacefully braiding her hair and avoiding even the appearance of work.

'Manchán,' she screamed, like it was his fault, but the wind changed direction and the gap closed again.

'Muck,' shouted Manchán, trying to catch the wall with his toes, 'grab onto my belt.'

But Muck hadn't learned that trick yet and instead stayed where he was, crouched in the shelter of the flapping door, shivering, both ears flattened down on either side of his head. Muck hated wind.

Beside Manchán, his mother appeared. It was a knack she had, of seeming to come out of nowhere, and she had often startled Manchán unpleasantly with it in the past. Now he was just extremely relieved to see her. With one hand she grabbed the edge of the net and pulled. With the other hand she stabbed a peg of wood into the soft hut wall and hauled backwards with all her weight until she could slip the net

over it. Then she hammered a second peg in on his other side and repeated the process.

'Can I let go now?' asked Manchán, checking, and his mother nodded. He dropped to the ground.

'Well done, pet,' shouted Manchán's father, hurrying around the hut. 'And well done, Manchán,' he added with a wink. 'I nearly thought we'd lost you there, the way the wind is blowing.'

Manchán puffed out his cheeks. That was exactly what he had been thinking as well, that and the difficult question of when exactly to let go. Too quickly, and he would have been blamed for the de-thatching of their home; too slowly and he'd have ended up as a hostage, or worse, in the kingdom beyond the river.

'Anyway,' Manchán's father continued, 'my idea worked, all credit to your mother.'

'Your idea,' said Manchán's mother, tying the net off with a hard knot onto the two pegs. 'What idea would that be?'

'About the net,' said Manchán's father, admiring

his handiwork. 'To keep the roof on.' He waved a hand in the general direction of the thatch.

'And what will you fish with?' asked Manchán's mother, not exactly admiring the roof, or her husband either.

'Well, pet ...' Manchán's father hesitated. 'It's just a test.

'A test?' asked Manchán's mother loudly. 'What sort of a test?'

'A test of an idea,' said Manchán's father. 'To test if the idea would work or not. And look,' he added brightly, 'it did.'

A sudden gust buffeted them and his eyes blinked anxiously at the roof. *If eyes could speak*, thought Manchán, *they'd be saying 'pleeease' right now.*

'And what's wrong with stitching the thatch on with willow rods?' asked Manchán's mother. 'Like everybody else does.'

'Because,' said Manchán's father, starting to sweat, 'I ran out of willow rods.'

'How can you run out of willow rods?' asked Manchán's mother. 'The countryside is infested with them.'

'I mean I ran out of the ones I had picked,' said Manchán's father, changing course. 'I used them.'

'For what?' said Manchán's mother.

'For a kind of basket.'

'What kind of basket?'

'A fishing basket.'

'A fishing basket?'

'A basket to catch fish in,' Manchán's father explained. 'It was another sort of an idea I had.'

Around them the wind rose to a screech or maybe it was his mother's brain-ball, thought Manchán. She wasn't the world's biggest supporter of new ideas, and especially not ones that emanated from her husband. He waited with interest to hear what his father would say next. So did his mother.

And now Méabh joined them as well, sort of, peering out through the door over Muck's head, her braids whipping in the gale like a knot of eels.

They all waited. Manchán's father looked from one family member to the next, while around them the wind rose to a high, fierce scream. He reminded Manchán of a hare he had once encountered, backed up against a stone wall, cornered by dogs. His mouth opened and closed but no sound came out, or maybe it did – it was hard to tell with the gale. Manchán's mother frowned. Clearly she couldn't hear anything either. She opened her mouth to speak and there was a sudden loud pop. The air filled with straw.

'Crom, Bríd agus Lugh,' shouted their neighbour's voice. 'Heeelp! Me roof is gone!'

Manchán shielded his eyes against the straw-sting in his face and turned to squint. The neighbour's roof was whirling in pieces around them. Further up the village there was another pop as a second roof exploded, the thatch torn to shreds by the wind's busy fingers. Then a great noise of bleating went up.

'My sheep!' boomed a voice. 'My sheep are loose.'

A second look flickered across Manchán's father's face. 'That's the chief,' he shouted. 'The wind must have blown down his enclosure. Quick!' And he turned and sprinted towards the tumult.

Manchán recognised this second look as well, and grinned. It was the same look as the hare when it turned and discovered a hole in the wall behind it. He sprinted after his father, and his mother followed. Behind them Méabh tried leaping over Muck and tripped.

'Muck,' she shouted, like it was his fault, then something else as well.

But Manchán didn't hear. He had turned the corner already and was forging ahead into the hard, funnelling gale.

The wind blasted and roared. To the left and right of him sheep were tumbling like tiny clouds blown from the sky. Bleating in panic, they scattered between the huts and fled into the wild country beyond. Manchán threw himself at one in passing and held on tight, his fingers digging deep into its thick, matted wool. Panicked by Manchán's assault and pushed by the wind from behind, the animal took off like a snipe exploding from cover.

'Trip the baste, Manchán,' shouted Pagan's grandfather, Fionn, emerging from behind a hut and tripping one of the woolly escapees before twisting it neatly to the ground by its back leg.

'That's the way to do it,' he roared, as Manchán was dragged violently past him, but of course Fionn had had more practice.

The sheep increased its speed. If Manchán had had time to think, he would have picked a smaller one, a lamb even, with fluffy woolly curls and dainty pointy hooves. Instead he had thrown himself at Balor, the chieftain's wicked old one-eyed bull sheep, a ram who had once taken on a wolf in single combat, and had driven its

horns so hard into the wolf's open mouth that the howl was heard in the next kingdom and a wolf's tooth had remained embedded in Balor's curly horn for ever after. It was where he had lost his eye as well, and gained his name. 'An eye for a tooth,' Brother Abstemius had commented mysteriously when he heard about the episode, an odd remark that nobody quite understood. They understood Balor, though, and dived out of his path as he charged like an army of one through the village, Manchán dangling from his back. The last man standing between them and the Tangled Forest beyond was the warrior Ruán the Ditherer.

Balor bore down balefully. Ruán dithered. Behind Balor the remaining sheep swerved like birds and charged after their leader.

'Get back here with my ram, Manchán,' roared the chieftain, like it was Manchán's fault.

And Ruán still dithered.

Balor lowered his horns and accelerated. His skull was massive and scarred from innumerable battles. He didn't care if somebody hesitated or

not. It made no difference as far as he was con-
cerned. When he got to Ruán, Ruán stopped
dithering and jumped. He jumped so high that
Balor and Manchán shot by underneath and
Manchán shouted, 'Good jump, Ruán.'

'Thanks, Manchán,' called Ruán and landed,
just in time to be trampled to the ground by
Balor's followers, bleating and jumping and
bumping into each other in a panicked attempt
to catch up with their leader and get quickly
away from the village and the awful coursing
gale.

Balor pounded on. His hooves crossed onto the soft turf marking the border of the village and churned it up into Manchán's face and hair. Manchán spat and gripped harder with his fingers. Briefly he considered swinging his legs down and trying to drag Balor's gallop to a trot, but a hoof caught him on the knee and changed his mind immediately. And what if he just simply let go? Well, he had seen what had happened to Ruán. On the other hand, he decided, if Balor headed for the river he would definitely let go. Before they hit the water anyway.

Instead, Balor hit a bump. He hit it hard with his front hooves and Manchán was flung briefly forward. He rose vertically on his arms like he was attempting a handstand on Balor's shoulders, and as Balor pushed off the bump, and galloped onward, Manchán was folded backwards and landed again, this time sitting upright on the ram's back.

'Crom's socks,' shouted Manchán's father. 'Look at Manchán go.'

And indeed, the whole village was looking. Straddled on Balor's back, riding him like a pony, Manchán galloped away pursued by the ragged remains of the chieftain's prize herd.

'Turn him, Manchán,' shouted some genius, 'turn the beast.'

Méabh snorted. 'You might as well try to turn the storm,' she remarked, and she was right.

Two breaths later Balor jumped over an old log and disappeared into a dip leading towards the far edge of the Tangled Forest. There was an extra-strong gust of wind, and a flurry of leaves fell like a curtain over the boy and the disappearing animals.

Back in the village the chieftain turned and glared at his warriors. 'Why didn't you stop them?' he shouted. The warriors shuffled and didn't reply. It was never wise to be the first to give an answer to the chieftain that he didn't want to hear.

'Well, why didn't *you* stop them?' said Manchán's mother, bristling. 'After all, they're your sheep.'

'*Were* your sheep,' added Méabh helpfully. 'Well it's true,' she said, when her father glared at her. 'I mean, they're gone now, aren't they?'

The chieftain swung towards them. He was nearly seven feet tall and, like Balor, covered in scars from battle. They crawled over his body like words from the Book of War. He would fight anybody, even his own shadow on a bloodmoon night, where a single injury might mean his own swift demise and a journey to the Land of the Ancestral Warriors, or, if Brother Abstemius was correct, to one of the two new places – heaven or hell as they were called – neither of which sounded particularly fun, and both of which seemed to go on for a very long time. Now he towered over Manchán's mother and glared. Glaring was another speciality of his. And Manchán's mother glared right back. She wasn't afraid of anybody, especially not a chieftain.

'Now, now,' said Manchán's father nervously, but the chieftain knew better than to tangle with Manchán's mother. Her tongue was sharper than his axe any day and left a more lasting mark, all the worse for being invisible.

'Fetch my hounds,' he shouted, backing up a step and disguising a retreat as a plan of action. 'We'll track them down and bring them back before nightfall.'

'Good luck with that,' said Méabh cheerfully and laughed. 'Knowing Manchán,' she added, 'you'll need it.'

The chieftain pretended not to hear her.

But Manchán himself could have done with a pinch of luck too, as Balor was still charging. The thing about Balor was that he was as tireless as he was smelly – more, even, if that were possible, thought Manchán, gagging slightly and still stuck limpet-tight to the galloping ram's back. But at least it was better than being dragged over the ground behind him and beaten with hooves. Just about!

And Balor had fleas! Manchán could feel

them, jumping at him as he jiggled, burrowing into his hair and tunic as he rode, and probably shouting *Yippee* in their little flea voices. He hadn't known that sheep had fleas, but maybe it was just a Balor speciality and one of his many secret weapons. Crom only knew what else he was hiding.

Manchán risked a glance behind. What was left of the flock was having a hard time keeping up, and the lazier ones among them had stopped as soon as they found shelter from the gale and a nice patch of grass. And who could blame them? Manchán himself would have been quite happy with a bit of shelter and a nice patch of grass to relax on. Instead he was racing the wind towards the Tangled Forest, where he had as much chance of staying on Balor's back as a summer without rain. The trees would see to that.

And why him? Why not Pagan or, better still, Méabh? Why did nothing ever happen to them? The length of one short song ago Manchán had been peacefully fixing the roof of the hut with Daddy, but now, unless he did something

quick, he was about to be swatted full force by
a knotted fist of oak and hurled senseless to the
ground. He gritted his teeth and pushed himself
up on his haunches. The Tangled Forest flung
up before him like a thousand pointed elbows.
He got ready to jump.

And Balor swerved.

Manchán sat back down again. He was starting to get the hang of things now. A saddle
would have been welcome, but who ever saw

a saddle on a sheep? And anyway, Balor had so much matted, twisty hair on his back that it was almost like sitting on a cushion – a very dangerous cushion stuffed with fleas and travelling at top speed over the grassy ground.

The ground turned stony. Manchán glanced to his right. The Tangled Forest still beckoned with its twiggy fingers but Balor had chosen a path that led right past it. Now he was aiming straight for the Great Bog of Squelch. The wind-noise behind them rose like the howling of hounds. As they entered the shelter of the tree line, Manchán realised that it was in fact the howling of hounds. They were being pursued.

The Great Bog of Squelch was called 'great' not as a compliment but on account of its size. Méabh, for example, called it the Horrible Bog of Squat, or worse if the parents weren't around to correct her. She never went there. And most other people avoided it too, sensible people anyway. You could sink in the bog or get lost for ever in one of its sudden mists.

And there were voices in the bog as well,

and lights and tricky fairies. Pagan's grandfather claimed he had twice been driven from the path by the Púca charging out of the night towards him while he was making his way home, completely sober. But Manchán didn't mind the bog and sometimes went there with Pagan to simply muck about or pick the cotton wisps or hunt for birds' eggs. He liked the sounds and the mists and the way the ground squeezed wetly between his toes and stained his feet brown for days afterwards. For the bog was beautiful, in its own boggy way, the air fragrant and full of butterflies, flitting scraps of colour against the dull umber landscape, with larks spiralling ever upwards, lifted by the beauty of their own exalted song. The exact opposite, in fact, of Balor, grunting and snorting over the ground and ploughing the mud up around him with his big, thumping hooves.

'Go on, Balor,' screamed Manchán, suddenly overcome by the immensity of the moment. Maybe the ram wasn't a delicate butterfly or a lovely tremulous lark but, by Crom, he was a great powerful beast in his own right, and who else from the village had ridden him this far or this fast – or ever, for that matter?

'Go on, Balor,' he shouted again, and dug his heels hard into Balor's sides to encourage him to go even faster. Instead Balor immediately braked and scraped wildly to a halt. He twisted his head and his one good eye swivelled angrily, then fixed on Manchán. The pupil contracted to the size of a pinhole and the eyeball gleamed most redly. Until now, Balor hadn't actually realised that somebody was clinging to his back and now that he had found out, he wasn't too happy about it either. With a great blasting snort, he threw himself forward onto his forelegs and kicked his hindquarters high into the air. Manchán clung on with the grip of a drowning man.

Balor bucked and bellowed. Like a frog dodging a heron he flung himself high into the air, flexing and straightening his back in an effort to shake off his annoying baggage. But Manchán held on tight with everything he could, including toes and teeth, and as long as Balor didn't think of simply rolling on the ground, Manchán started to hope that he might outlast him. After all, he had stayed on this far, hadn't he?

Behind them on the ridge, a movement, and the chieftain's trio of huge hounds appeared. They were large and grey and hairy, wolfhounds all three, and scarier than wolves any day. But then, so was Balor. They stopped on the ridge and howled to let their master and the rest of the village know that they had found their

prey. Not that that was very difficult, thought Manchán, his brain-ball slamming around inside his skull. For Balor had left a track behind him like a deep ploughed furrow that everybody could follow.

And follow they did. It seemed to Manchán, between leaps and bucks, that the entire village was now assembling to watch his humiliation, heads appearing one after another over the ridge, and well out in front, making sure she had the best view of all, his sister Méabh.

'Come on, Manchán,' she called sarcastically, and Manchán gritted his teeth and wound his fingers tighter into Balor's wool. *Not now*, he prayed. *Not while Méabh is watching.*

'A pot of ale on Balor to throw Manchán,' shouted a voice. That was Brian Brew, the beer-master.

'I'll take that bet,' called Pagan's grandfather, 'and double it. Up Manchán!'

'Two pots,' shouted Brian. 'Go on, Balor. Shake the boyo off!'

'A comb of honey and some fine beeswax on

Manchán,' called Bacmala the beekeeper.

'A leather girth and two pearl buttons on Balor.'

'A smoked eel and four hooks on Manchán.'

'A horn to call with and the handle of a sword on Balor.'

'A fishing basket on Manchán.'

'What's a fishing basket?' asked Ruán the Ditherer, and Manchán's father explained.

'I'll have to think about it,' said Ruán.

Then the chieftain let out a roar. 'My house, my sheep, my sword, all on Balor,' he said.

'Against what?' asked Méabh.

'Service in my house for a year and a day,' answered the chieftain.

'Done,' said Méabh and spat in her hand for him to shake.

'You can't serve in the chieftain's house,' snapped her mother. 'I need you at home.'

'Not me,' said Méabh turning pale. 'I meant Manchán.'

But the chieftain just grinned.

'Too late,' he shouted, and turned his face towards the battle.

'COME ON, BALOR!' he cried.

'COME ON, MANCHÁN!' screamed Méabh. And this time, she really meant it.

Balor leapt and bucked. By now he had moved into the bog and was jumping from rock to rock, his hard hooves knocking sparks as he landed with the force of heavy hammer blows. It felt to Manchán like somebody was shaking him in the air while battering his behind with a hurley stick at the same time. If the bog was Balor, thought the last thinking corner of Manchán's mind, then Balor was the flea springing about on the bog's back, but who was Manchán? Then he stopped thinking as Balor paused for breath

at the edge of a stubby cliff, heart heaving, legs splayed like a hand. In the silence that followed, faint calling voices could be heard. *Up Balor*, they shouted, but *Up Manchán* as well, and for a moment Manchán clearly heard the voice of his own mother calling, 'Come on, Manchán. Show that old ram who's really in charge.'

Well, he was trying, he thought. Nobody could claim otherwise. He stared out over the cliff edge and gulped. Then he swallowed his gulp as Balor stamped twice on the ground,

snapped all four legs straight and took off like a rock fired from a sling.

The bog flew by beneath them. Manchán could see exactly what Balor was aiming for. It was a boulder in the middle of a particularly squelchy spot of bog. From there he could spring to a path before galloping off into the mist, bucking and leaping and annoying the fairies who would probably take it out on Manchán. It was a mighty jump and one that Balor would normally have made easily. Only 'normally' didn't include a small boy clinging tightly to his back. When Balor straightened his legs this time and jumped, he didn't account for that tiny little bit of extra weight. With the noise of a bare foot driving into a cowpat, he landed instead in the bog, the length of one arm away from his target, and sank to the shoulder. Caught like a wasp in honey, he threw back his enormous head and bellowed.

'Go on and bellow, you old ram,' said Manchán cheerfully, 'for that's all you can do.'

Then he waited for the village to arrive at the edge of the cliff, his supporters chanting his name, and the ones who had bet against him as well.

And when they were all assembled and watching, he stepped lightly from Balor's back, up onto his horns and from there onto the rock which the leaping ram had missed by an infinite whisper. Then with everybody cheering, and especially his father, but even Méabh and his mother clapping in time, he threw up his arms in the air and did a quick and lively jig of triumph.

CHAPTER FIVE

n which Manchán and Pagan set out to go Fishing. Pagan's Grandfather Fionn-of-the-Question. The Tangled Forest. Birdsong and a Song from Manchán. A strange Encounter. Frogs' Milk and Spirals.

It was a fine, bright morning and Manchán and Muck were following the path to the hut where Pagan lived with his grandfather Fionn-of-the-Question. The path curled through the village like the stroke of a pen and ended in a hollow just before the Tangled Forest. From there the path split like the fingers on a hand with one digit each for the four great provinces of Ireland and the thumb for the Old Kingdom where the Other People lived. Fionn had been down that path and back many times, according to himself, but Manchán had yet to be tempted. For one thing, it was dark and twisty, even in high summer, and for another, it was silent, and this back in the days when the air was drenched in birdsong.

'Birdsong,' said Manchán's father, holding up a finger, 'is the sound of Heaven heard in our world.'

'Even seagulls?' asked Méabh.

'Well, maybe not seagulls,' agreed her father.

'And what about crows?' said Méabh.

'Or crows,' said her father, 'but most other birds.'

'And chickens?' said Méabh. 'What would you say about chickens?'

'I would say, "Have you fed them yet?"' answered her father, putting an end to what, knowing Méabh, could be a very long list of counter-examples.

'That's Méabh all right,' said Pagan, when Manchán told him about the conversation, 'always pushing things just a little bit too far.'

Manchán agreed.

Now they were sitting outside Pagan's grand-father's hut watching him work. Fionn was a stonecutter. He took a hard bit of rock and he used it to chisel patterns into a softer bit of rock. Mostly the patterns were a sort of spiral, or a spiral within a spiral. Or sometimes they were three spirals together in a kind of a triangle, with curly bits at each corner. Only lately, with the monastery being built on the shore of the lake, was he getting around to doing square things, with crosses and lines, but they were more difficult.

'What does the spiral mean?' asked Manchán once, while he and Pagan were skinning a rabbit they had caught together.

Fionn answered, 'Why does it have to mean anything?'

Manchán said, 'So it's just a kind of a pattern, then?'

And Fionn had answered, 'What do *you* think it is?'

Fionn was notorious for answering questions with a question of his own, a sign of great wisdom according to some, or early softening of the brain, according to many. But Manchán liked Pagan's grandfather, and he liked chatting to him, and he liked his spirals as well. Even if they didn't mean anything, they *seemed* to mean something, and wasn't that enough sometimes?

'Well, what's this one?' asked Manchán now, pointing at a drawing scratched onto a flat slate propped against the hut. It showed a tall high cross with a circle at the top where the arms extended.

'That's a bit of an idea I had for the monks,' said Fionn. 'Including your uncle Abstemius,' he added. 'He's coming to look at it next week.'

'It's nice,' said Manchán, and Fionn nodded.

'I couldn't make it work with a spiral but sure the circle will do. Now, boys, I'll let you get on with your work and I'll get on with mine. What d'ye say?'

And they said yes of course, especially as it wasn't exactly work they were getting on with, but only a sort of work, otherwise known as fishing. Manchán and Pagan were going mucking about on the river. It had rained heavily over the last few weeks and the water was deep and smooth and full. There was a spot at a bend that Pagan knew, where the river had risen into the meadow and flooded through a copse of trees. The current was quiet in this spot and Pagan was sure that they would find trout there, suspended silently in the sun-dappled water, just waiting for him and Manchán to come along.

'We can sit in the trees,' he said, 'and haul them up with both fists. Then we'll make a fire

and eat our fill before we even think about carrying the rest home.'

Manchán grinned while the waters in his
mouth rose like the river. If there was anything
tastier than a fresh-grilled trout, he had yet to
try it. He opened his mouth and tried out a
song that had just popped into his head.

When Pagan went down to the river that day,
The birds began to sing.
Take heed of the lad with the rod in his hand,
He'll hook you on a string.
But the trout they didn't listen,
And the birdsong went unheard.
For who ever heard of a fish with ears,
And … something something … bird.

He couldn't think of a last line so he went
back for another try.

For a fish with ears was never yet seen
… something something -een.

It still wouldn't work.

'I'll have to think about it for a bit,' he said, and Pagan laughed. Manchán was good at coming up with songs, just like his father. And who knew, maybe one day he would be even better. Then anybody he made a song about would be famous, or laughed at. That's why people said it was always good to stay on the side of the singers.

The boys pushed on. Pagan had wanted to go around the Tangled Forest but Manchán suggested taking the north road, a path really, winding up a short hill from where they could cut down easily towards the river, and a great short-cut, according to his father. At least Manchán was fairly sure it was the north road he had mentioned.

Now the sun was above and behind their backs, shining greenly through the leafy canopy overhead and throwing a flickering shadow before them. The ground under their feet was giving and soft like a carpet, a thing they had heard of though never actually seen, and a pleasure to walk on. Even Muck seemed to like it, but then he enjoyed walking on pretty much anything. He went trotting ahead with a little extra bounce in each step.

He snuffled and snorted and stopped from time to time to check that Manchán and his pal were keeping up with him. And of course they were. People were good at walking back then, much better than now, and had lots of practice too, since walking was the main way of getting around.

They walked on. The ground grew bumpy. The forest in those days was not as neat and tidy as it is now. They jumped over a fallen branch and ducked under a tree that was cracked right down the middle and looked like it had been split by a giant axe.

'Lightning,' said Pagan. 'That must have been some sight.'

'Or a giant woodpecker,' said Manchán, and laughed. 'That would be an even greater sight.'

He whacked a branch with a stick he had found on the wayside. The sound cracked in the glade and the birds fell silent. 'Manchán,' said Pagan crossly, 'ssshh.' But Manchán ignored him. He had found some tall nettles to do battle with. *Whack whack whack*, and victory was his. And every time he struck, the birdsong stopped for a moment, then started up again.

The path grew narrower. The boys walked in single file with Manchán taking up the rear. A narrow path was one that was rarely used, or maybe only used by animals, though which animals? A reasonable question in the days when wolves wandered the woods. Behind Pagan, Manchán had commenced whistling. Manchán was a noisy person, compared to Pagan anyway, who was more on the quiet side. When Manchán wasn't chatting, he was singing, and when he wasn't singing, he was whistling. Or whacking nettles. It could be a bit distracting at times, and this was one of those times.

'Manchán,' said Pagan, 'would you be quiet for a second and listen!'

Manchán stopped whistling. 'What's wrong?' he asked.

Pagan didn't answer, just raised a hand. Then he whispered, 'The birdsong.'

'What about it?'

'There isn't any,' said Pagan.

Manchán looked around. A wood could be a loud place if you knew what to listen for, a thicket of subtle sounds, most of which Manchán knew. There were the birds, of course, and the animals big and small, and the insects, but even the trees made different noises, or spoke according to some. Now the silence was stifling and it felt as if the forest was holding its breath and turning towards them. Manchán's stomach squeezed. He didn't like the feeling one little bit. It reminded him of the time when he ate a mussel that had opened up a tiny bit too easily. Then something bumped against his legs and shoved hard between them. 'Muck,' said Manchán, startled, and Muck's tail drooped unhappily. Whatever it was the boys sensed, he sensed it too.

Above their heads a flurry of wind brushed the tree canopy and a shaft of light stabbed through to the shadowy brush below. It lit a watching figure a little way off. The figure was tall and thin, with arms and shining eyes and antlers growing from its head. The arms meant it wasn't a deer.

'Crom's socks,' squeaked Pagan, his hair standing straight up on his head, but Manchán had seen it too. With Pagan leading the way and

Muck three paces behind, they lifted their legs and ran.

It's not easy to run in a forest, and back then it was even harder, almost impossible really, what with brambles to grab you and branches to trip you up. The only good way to run was to stick to your path, but the path seemed to have disappeared under their feet. Instead of escaping they were getting tangled up in the roots and twigs of the trees that gave the forest its name, and not getting very far at all.

'Quick,' shouted Manchán, 'follow Muck,' and indeed that was a good idea. Muck was small but strong and easily capable of ploughing a compact path through the undergrowth. He pushed ahead and the boys followed as fast as they could in his footsteps.

And as they ran the forest grew darker. It was a green dark now, the kind that happens when the trees grow so old they are like giant hands blocking the sun. They were hard to run around, with their wide massive trunks and vast wealed roots, but it wasn't like the boys had a choice.

'Muck,' shouted Manchán, 'aim for the river.'
He hoped Muck heard, though even if he heard
he might not understand. You didn't always
know with pigs.

Up ahead, another gust of wind, and the sun
struck greenly through the canopy once more.
For the second time the horned figure appeared
before them in a shaft of light, both arms spread
out this time, with large fingery hands at each
end, like somebody wanting to give them a
horrible hug.

'Aghhh,' shouted Pagan and veered so
strongly left that he nearly skidded.

'Aaaahhhh,' shouted Manchán, accelerating
past him.

'Ooof,' grunted
the figure as
Muck, too late
to stop, ran
straight into its
middle. There
was a crack as
one of the antlers

snapped and the figure sat down hard.

'Muck,' shouted Manchán. Then his foot caught on Pagan and the ground gave way beneath them. They tumbled nose first into a hole.

The thing about falling, thought Manchán as he fell, *is that it's over in a second, but while it's going on, it seems to take ages.*

Then he landed. Hard!

'Ouch,' said Manchán, and it felt like his voice was coming from somebody else, a great big somebody else pressing down hard on top of him. He realised it was actually coming from somebody else.

'Pagan,' he said loudly, 'get off me.'

'I'm trying,' said Pagan just as loudly. 'Stop wriggling.'

'I'm not wriggling,' said Manchán.

'Well, something is wriggling,' said Pagan, 'and it's not me.'

'It's Paddy,' said a high sing-song voice above them. 'Yer squashing him. And Paddy hates being squashed.'

'Who's Paddy?' said Manchán, alarmed.

From beneath them, a small wicked head with bright green eyes and an orange forked tongue slid between him and Pagan and floated under their noses like an eel in water.

'Now, Paddy,' said the voice from above, 'behave yourself.'

Later on, Manchán wasn't sure how they had done it, but he and Pagan erupted from the hole like spray through a sea spout. And so might you, if you found yourself sitting on a large and twisty snake.

'Hee hee hee,' said the sing-song voice, as they blasted past him before coming to a hard landing on the forest floor. 'Paddy won't hurt you. Not unless you annoy him.'

Manchán looked at the voice. It was coming from a long hairy bush, with flowers and leaves sprouting from it and arms and a single horn on top. One of the arms was hooked around Muck's tummy, though he didn't seem unhappy about it. The other arm held a broken antler, which must have been the crack they heard. And from the middle of the bush, a nose and two bright eyes of different colours stared at them. It wasn't a bush at all.

'Now boys,' said Mothall the druid, 'is it visiting me you are, or just passing through?'

Manchán and Pagan jumped to their feet. 'We're just passing through, said Pagan, and added quickly, 'Your Honour.' The druids were a touchy lot and it was always sensible to be a little bit extra polite around them.

'And will you not stay for a cup of milk,' said Mothall, 'and a chat?'

'We won't,' said Pagan, 'but many thanks.'

'Are you sure?' said Mothall. 'It's lovely fresh milk and nice and cool on a hot day like today.'

'We're sure,' said Pagan, frowning at Manchán,

who was now staring at Muck, pink-cheeked and wheezing slightly under Mothall's arm. Was Mothall tickling him? Was that why he looked so happy?

'It's no bother at all,' said Mothall, 'and the fish aren't going anywhere.'

'How did you know we were going fi–' started Manchán, then he stopped. That was the druids for you, always a step or two ahead.

'Well, sure, if you don't want to, then I won't keep you,' said Mothall, 'but thanks for the pig.'

Manchán turned pale. 'A cup of milk would be nice,' he said quickly before Pagan refused again.

Mothall's eyes twinkled. 'Grand,' he said, and lowered Muck to the ground. 'I was only joking about your pig,' he added. 'Sure, that would make Paddy jealous.'

He stuck the broken horn crookedly back onto his head and turned to go. Like a pale finger of moonlight sliding over the forest floor, Paddy twisty-slithered between Manchán's feet and disappeared up into the druid's tangled garment. For a second it looked like Mothall had sprouted a tail, but then, there were so many things dangling and tangling about him, one more hardly made a difference.

The druids are a funny lot, thought Manchán, following behind. According to his father they swam like the salmon both backwards and forwards in time and were able, if they wanted, to remember the future. His mother said they were a scruffy, rubbishy lot who spent way too much time by themselves and who didn't have half the knowledge of herbs that she did. But she agreed that they were best avoided if possible.

She wouldn't be pleased, thought Manchán, if she knew what he was up to now, but as that was generally the case, he was able to put it out of his mind and concentrate on getting out of the situation.

'One cup of milk,' he whispered to Pagan, 'and we'll be on our way.'

Pagan nodded. He knew that Manchán wouldn't leave without Muck and he wasn't going to leave without Manchán. And anyway, the day was warm and the fish would wait and a nice cold cup of milk was a fine thing in and of itself.

'It's frog's milk,' called Mothall over his shoulder. 'I milked them myself this morning.'

They reached the lightning tree, or at least a tree that looked liked the lightning tree, though only from behind. When they passed it, the other side was somehow still intact. Mothall patted the trunk and scrambled quickly over its roots. Then he pushed through a screen of

nettles and into a clearing. In the middle of the clearing there was a large flat stone with smaller rocks arranged in a circle around it.

'Take the weight off your legs,' said Mothall, 'and I'll fetch the milk. Would you like a biscuit to go with it?'

'What sort of biscuit?' asked Manchán cautiously. The frog's milk sounded bad enough.

'An oatie biscuit,' said Mothall, 'with honey.'

'That sounds nice,' said Manchán, relieved.

'I bake them myself,' said Mothall, and Pagan said, 'Doesn't everybody?'

'True,' said Mothall, 'but one day most people will buy their oatie biscuits in small expensive quantities, already wrapped in thin waterproof parcels of all colours. And not only that, there will be many different kinds of oatie biscuit too.'

Manchán stifled a laugh and looked at Pagan. The next time they would definitely go around the woods, he thought, and to Crom with shortcuts. If the wolves or the fairies didn't get you, you'd end up drinking frogs' milk with a lunatic

and his pet snake. And that wasn't a whole lot better.

He looked down at Mothall's stone table. Its surface was covered in deeply etched spirals, all connected to each other, and he thought he recognised the handiwork.

'That's your grandfather's mark,' he said to Pagan, who nodded.

'Grandad supplies most of the druids,' he said. 'They're fond of his spirals.'

'They're nice,' agreed Manchán, running his hand over the rough surface.

'*Nice!*' said Mothall, coming back with a cup in each hand. 'They're more than nice. The spiral is everything, boys, and don't you forget it. Now, here's to your health,' and he put the cups in front of them.

Manchán looked at the cup. At least the milk wasn't green, he thought. And it smelled normal too. But still!

'What do you mean the spiral is everything?' he asked, delaying the moment when he'd have to drink, but also because he was genuinely curious. At least Mothall didn't seem to be the type to answer a question with a question. He was more the garrulous kind of person.

'The spiral is the path of life,' explained Mothall, leaving his audience no clearer than they had been. But he was only getting started. 'On a spiral you can go forwards and backwards or inwards and outwards or round and round, all at the same time,' he explained. 'You can be at the edge of things or in the middle of things. You can see before you and behind you. All life is in the spiral. It is one of our most ancient and potent symbols. Sláinte,' he added politely, and raised his cup.

Manchán frowned, not quite sure if that was the explanation or not. 'The spiral looks a bit like a snake,' he said.

'Oh, it does,' said Mothall. 'Or a worm. But you can't take a worm seriously, so a snake is your only man. There's nothing like a snake for getting people's attention.'

As he spoke, his beard parted and Paddy's head nosed out. Pagan, Manchán and Muck all immediately looked at him, especially Muck, with a wary piggy eye, and who could blame him? Snakes are quite fond of pigs.

What an odd creature a snake is, thought Manchán, looking at Paddy, a mouth attached to a tail with two hard little emeralds to see with and an orange tongue flickering like a weak flame around his nostrils. *No wonder they make people uneasy.*

'Why do you call him Paddy?' he asked, and Mothall cackled. 'After my great rival,' he said, 'the fella with the sham-rocks and the horrible accent. He has a great fear

of snakes so I did it to annoy him. And snakes don't care what you call them because they've no ears to hear you with. Like fish. Isn't that right, Paddy?' He scratched Paddy's chin with a thumbnail and Paddy slid back into Mothall's beard. 'Paddy's from Egypt,' he said. 'Cost me an arm and a leg, but sure what can you do? There's no snakes in Ireland. Now, back to the spiral,' he said. 'Did you understand what I told you?'

'No,' said Pagan, and Manchán agreed.

'A line has a beginning and an end,' said Mothall, 'and that's it. A circle goes around and around and that's it. But a spiral has a bit of everything to it. Now do you see?'

'Sort of,' said Manchán, and Pagan nodded.

'Look,' said Mothall. 'Here's you.'

He placed a long fingernail in a middle whorl of one of the spirals on the table. 'If you go this way,' he explained, 'the spiral will take you in towards the centre. That's your fate and there's no avoiding it, even if you think there is. And at the same time, you can see where you are coming from and where you are going to. With practice, you can see it all at the same time.'

'Like you?' said Manchán.

'Like me,' said Mothall.

'Is that how you knew we were going fishing?' asked Pagan.

'I knew you were going fishing because of your fishing rods,' said Mothall.

'Right,' said Pagan.

'And do you know if we will catch anything?' said Manchán, grinning a bit at Pagan.

'You will,' said Mothall and closed his eyes. 'Bigger than a fish,' he chanted, 'and only after a hard struggle. On your hook it will be, but you'll go home hungry.'

Manchán considered this while he reached for another oatie biscuit. They were very nice, he thought, and if he was going to go home hungry, then he should at least try to eat as many as possible. Pity about the stupid milk.

'By the way,' said Mothall suddenly, 'watch out for turnips.'

'Who?' said Manchán.

'You,' said Mothall. 'There's turnips in your future, many turnips. But other things too.' He closed his eyes and concentrated. 'Small armies of ants,' he chanted, 'marching on inky feet over pages of white, all carrying meaning, and coloured pictures too, lovely to behold. By the hand of the uncle who visits. I'm just mentioning it.' Then he opened his eyes and held up a finger. 'Whisht,' he said, 'did you hear that?'

Manchán sneaked a look at Pagan. The longer they sat with Mothall, the weirder everything got. He could see that Pagan was thinking the same. It was definitely time to go.

'Well,' began Pagan, 'thanks for the hospitality, er … Your Honour,' but Mothall ignored him. Instead his ear was turned towards the path with his head cocked like a bird. From the distance they could hear somebody coming, two somebodies it sounded like, strolling through the woods, carrying with them the murmur of conversation and song, then the thwacking noise of a branch being struck. The birds fell silent. *Whack, whack, whack,* came the noise again, followed by the sound of whistling, a boy's whistling and another boy's voice telling him to be quiet for a second and listen. Pagan and Manchán glanced uneasily at each other.

'I think I know who that is,' said Mothall, 'but I'll just go and check.' He jumped up from his seat.

Pagan looked at Manchán and Manchán looked at Muck. It was now or never.

Above their heads a flurry of wind parted the leaves and a shaft of light opened onto the table below. Mothall's sing-song voice floated back towards them over the nettles. 'I was only joking about the milk,' he said, but the boys were up and running. Behind them an upturned cup spilled whitely into the deep-cut spirals and filled them in all directions before flowing off onto the forest floor below.

PAGAN'S SONG

When Pagan went down to the river that day
The birds began to sing,
Take heed of the boy with the rod in his hand
He'll catch you on a string.
With a fal-diddle dee, and a fal-diddle da,
Come on, the bould young Pagan.

When Pagan went up to the meadow that day
The hares began to leap,
Stay clear of the lad with the net in his hand
He'll trap you in your sleep.
With a fal-diddle dee, and a fal-diddle da,
Get up, the bould young Pagan.

When Pagan went into the woods that day
The deer began to low,
Beware of the boy with the flashing hand
He'll strike you with his bow.
With a fal-diddle dee, and a fal-diddle da,
Come on, the bould young Pagan.

When Pagan returned to the village that night
The shadows were deep and long.
With wile and will he had caught his fill,
I caught him with a song.
With a fal-diddle dee, and a fal-diddle da,
He is the bould young Pagan.

CHAPTER SIX

n which Manchán goes Fishing with Pagan and Méabh shows up and disturbs the Peace. A King Fish and an unexpected Catch. An End and a Beginning too.

anchán sat in a tree and dozed. The tree stood to its waist in water, the result of the rain that had lifted the river from its bed and spread it up over the sandy

bank where the rabbits lived. Now the rabbits had moved to the meadow beyond and the fish were gathered at the abandoned warren, the brown-freckled trout almost invisible under the light-sprinkled surface, with the smaller silver fish flickering around them like quartz.

According to Pagan, there was a pike in the warren too, a big fellow who had moved in with the flood, and if he stayed there after the river went back down, what a shock those rabbits were going to get! But Manchán wasn't interested in pike. For one thing, they always looked so appalled when you caught them, as if they took it personally, and for another, they were full of bones. Like pollock of the river, said his father, only harder to catch. But a trout, well, a trout was a different order of thing. Still, dozing was nice too, he thought, leaning back on his comfy branch. Already the world was receding from him and the door to the Land of Dreams was starting to open.

'Pagan,' came a girl's voice over the water, and the door slammed shut instantly. Manchán opened his eyes and groaned. In the tree beside him Pagan was dangling a line on the water and twitching it slightly to make it mimic a struggling fly and draw in a fish. He hadn't heard the voice at all.

'Pagan,' called Méabh again, louder this time, and now Pagan looked around. Better so, for the next thing Méabh would do would be to fire a stone at him to get his attention, and Méabh had a good aim.

'What is it?' he called.

'Have you seen Manchán?' asked Méabh.

She was standing on the other side of the river, and the trunk of the tree was between her and her brother, sheltering him from her view. Pagan looked at Manchán who shook his head vigorously.

'I haven't,' lied Pagan. 'Maybe he's off picking berries or something.'

'I was told he was with you,' said Méabh. 'That's what I heard.'

'He was here,' said Pagan, 'but he wasn't having any luck, and so he left again. Maybe he's further down the river.'

Méabh looked up and down the river. 'Manchán is horrible at fishing,' she announced. 'And he's not too good at picking berries either.'

'That's true,' said Pagan, grinning at Manchán's face. 'But he's good at singing.'

'Hmmph,' said Méabh, 'there's many better.' Then she sat down on the grass and dipped her feet in the water.

Pagan looked at her uneasily. 'Well, I won't keep you,' he said hopefully, but Méabh ignored the hint. Instead she put a hand in her hair and wound a few locks into a curl.

'Pagan,' she said, 'do you think I have nice hair?'

Pagan froze. Behind the tree trunk Manchán's eyes widened and he put two fingers into his mouth like he was on the verge of throwing up.

'Well?' said Méabh. 'Do you?'

'I suppose,' said Pagan, turning bright red.

'Very nice or just ordinary nice?' said Méabh, and Manchán jammed his fist into his mouth to keep from laughing. She was worse than a pike, his sister, once she bit. And Pagan's face was just brilliant.

'Well?' asked Méabh again. 'Which is it?'

'Very nice,' said Pagan, looking at the river. After all, what else could he say?

Then he put a hand over his mouth as if he was coughing and whispered, 'She can't swim, can she?'

Manchán shook his head. Méabh supported the idea of swimming, but she couldn't actually swim herself.

'Thank Crom,' said Pagan, who definitely did not want Méabh swimming over to his side of the river.

Méabh asked, 'What did you say?'

'I was just thanking Crom that my cough had stopped,' said Pagan feebly. *Cough cough*, he exaggerated, and Méabh looked at him carefully.

'Well,' she said, 'I think I'll just wait here quietly until Manchán returns.'

Manchán rolled his eyes and his shoulders slumped.

'But he might be ages,' said Pagan quickly. 'You know the way he gets distracted.'

'Indeed I do,' said Méabh, as if Manchán was a source of complete torture to her, instead of the other way round. 'But at least I'll have you to keep me company in the meantime.' She smiled.

Now Pagan's shoulders slumped. 'But won't it be boring for you?' he said. 'Just sitting there?'

'Most things are boring for me,' said Méabh, twirling her hair again, 'but I have learned to put up with them.'

Beyond the tree, a wind stirred, ruffling the glossy surface of the river. Under Manchán's branch, something big slid out of the shadows. *A salmon*, thought Manchán, leaning slightly to one side to get a better look. If there was one thing better than a trout, it was a salmon. He caught Pagan's eye and pointed with his nose. Pagan looked at him and frowned. He clearly had no idea what Manchán was on about. Plus, he had other problems on his mind right now. Below him, the lure dangled forgotten in the water.

'Pagan,' said Méabh loudly, 'why are you frowning at the tree?'

'I'm not,' said Pagan. 'I'm just thinking.'

'Are you thinking about me?' said Méabh, and the salmon struck.

Now for those of you who have yet to catch a salmon, imagine trying to reel in a medium-sized dog while the dog is pulling and jerking and running back and forth through bushes and all the time doing its best to get away from you. And then imagine that the line is delicate and could snap any moment, so you have to be careful not to put too much pressure on it. And lastly imagine doing all of this from the branch of a tree,  and now you have the situation Manchán and Pagan were in.

'Crom's socks,' shouted Manchán and grabbed at the rod while the line tumbled into the water below.

'Manchán, you cowpat,' screamed Méabh from her side of the riverbank, 'I knew you were there!'

'I'm on it,' roared Pagan, and grabbed at the line, which started burning through his fingers.

'Hold him!' shouted

Manchán, bracing himself on the branch, his toes digging into the bark while he balanced.

'I'm holding, I'm holding!' shouted Pagan. And the line went slack.

The boys looked around.

'Have you lost him?' shouted Méabh. 'Where is he?'

But Manchán couldn't tell. He tugged at the line, now hanging slackly in the water.

'I knew it,' shouted Méabh. 'You've lost him.'

'Is there anything you don't know?' retorted Manchán, taking his eye off the prize for one second.

With a sound like ripping cloth, the line tore through the water as the salmon took off like a spear hurled in battle.

Pagan howled as his fingers burned, and he let go of the line. On his branch Manchán stood up and braced for impact. And the impact came. With a tug that loosened his teeth, the salmon jerked him from his branch and he landed flat and painfully on the water below. The last thing he saw before his skull knocked against the sandy bottom were the small silver fish exploding in all directions and the head of the old pike poking out through one of the bigger rabbit holes. It looked like it was grinning.

Ha ha ha, laughed Méabh, the first sound Manchán heard when he broke the surface again and he knew he'd be hearing about this episode for a long time afterwards. The time the fish caught Manchán. *Ha ha ha!* And even Pagan was grinning, the cowpat. *Ha ha ha!* Everybody except Manchán having a great time altogether. And not just that, but they'd be going home hungry too. He thought about Mothall's prediction. What had he chanted again? *On your hook it will be. Bigger than a fish it will be.* Something about a hard struggle and then going home hungry. How annoying was all that, and what else did the future have in store for him?

Manchán splashed to the bank and pulled

himself out of the water. Muck came down to the lapping edge and nuzzled at him. *At least someone isn't laughing at me*, thought Manchán and closed his eyes against the sun shining through the trees. It was warm on his face, but also cool in places where the leaves blocked it. *How lovely both things are,* he thought, *how well they go together!* He shook his head hard and Muck ran away grunting at the water drops.

Then Manchán started laughing at himself too. What a sight he must have been, a boy pulled into the water by a fish! But what a fish that must have been as well! A king fish at least, to be able to do a deed like that. Tomorrow

he would come back again with Pagan and a stronger line this time, and no Méabh, and maybe then the luck would be with them. It was well known that some people had lots of luck while others went thirsty. But it was also well known that a person's luck could change, and often when it was least expected. Manchán could feel a change of luck coming at him now. There was no doubt about it.

'What was it you wanted to tell me?' he called across to Méabh.

And Méabh answered, 'Mother said you are to come home and take a bath.'

'A bath?' said Manchán, surprised. He almost never took a bath. Nobody did back then.

'And you need a haircut too,' said Méabh. 'That's what she told me.'

'A haircut?' said Manchán. 'What for?'

'Brother Abstemius is coming to collect you,' said Méabh, 'and Mother says you have to appear presentable.'

Manchán scowled and said nothing.

'She's even made you a new tunic,' said Méabh,

'with matching socks. Which is more than she ever made for me,' she added with a sniff.

'You can have mine,' said Manchán, 'and welcome. Because I won't be needing them.' Then he stood up to leave. 'Come on, Muck,' he said. 'This story is over and a new one is just beginning. Let's go.'

Méabh rubbed her hands together and laughed. 'You're my witness, Pagan,' she said. 'You heard him. Goodbye, Manchán,' she called, 'and thanks for the socks. I hope you get further than the next field this time.'

Manchán scowled. How was it she never got tired making fun of him? That was at least one thing he wouldn't miss.

'Goodbye, Pagan,' he said. 'You can keep my fishing rod. I'll return when I'm rich and famous.'

'So obviously never,' said Méabh cheerfully.

'Wait, Manchán,' said Pagan. 'Don't do anything rash.'

'And keep an eye out for flying turnips,' called Méabh. 'Just in case.'

Manchán scowled again. 'I've changed my mind about the socks,' he said. 'Pagan can have them, not you.'

'Too late,' said Méabh. 'They're no longer yours to give.' And she kicked the water with her dangling feet in his direction.

'I'll tell our mother,' said Manchán furiously, 'before I leave, I'll tell her. And that will sort you out.'

Méabh laughed again. 'You can tell her now if you want,' she said. 'She's right behind you.'

Manchán turned and looked. Their mother was making her way towards him down through the grassy meadow, walking quickly as she always did. The meadow was embraced by the river's arm and Manchán stood in the crook of the elbow. There was no escape possible. As soon as he could, thought Manchán, he would learn to swim and take his chances with the water fairies.

'Méabh,' said his mother, stopping a little distance away. 'Did you give Manchán my message?'

'I did,' said Méabh piously. 'Ages ago. But he has other plans and won't be needing his socks either, or so he informed me. Pagan is my witness.'

'Wait a second,' said Pagan.

'Méabh,' said their mother, 'go home.'

'But ...' said Méabh.

'And take Pagan with you,' said their mother.

Méabh smiled. 'All right, then,' she said. 'Come on, Pagan.'

'Wait a second,' said Pagan again, then his face brightened. 'I can't swim,' he lied. 'Sorry,

Méabh,' he called, 'I'll have to go the long way home.' And he jumped quickly from his branch to the riverbank, and ran for his life.

'Pagan,' shouted Méabh from the other side of the river, and belted after him.

Their mother shook her head, but made no move to interfere.

I'm for it now, thought Manchán.

His mother looked at her son and sat down on the grass.

'I am going to tell you something, Manchán,' she said, 'and I want you to hear me out.'

Nothing new in that, thought Manchán. She was always telling him things and forcing him to hear her out.

His mother said, 'And when I am finished,

you can make up your own mind what to do, and I won't stop you one way or another.'

Manchán paused. Now that was a new thing. At least, if she stuck to what she promised, it would be new.

'All right,' he said, 'tell me.'

'There is everything in the world,' began his mother, 'and everything in-between. Even in our small corner of it, we have our fill of dangers and pleasures and wonders. There is nothing like the world. And we are in the middle of it. Do you see what I mean?'

'I don't,' said Manchán truthfully, thinking, *Crom's socks, what is she getting at, at all, and where else would we be if not in the world?* It sounded to him more like his father speaking than his mother. His way was to go around the bush while her method was mostly to beat a path straight through it.

'I mean,' said his mother, 'that the world is always coming at us, in good ways and some-times in bad ways too. It is best if we are prepared for both.'

'What does this have to do with monking?' asked Manchán impatiently, and his mother frowned.

'I'm getting to it,' she answered sharply, 'if you don't keep interrupting me. Now whisht and listen.'

Manchán whishted. She sounded more like his mother again.

'A year is nothing at your age,' she said, 'though it seems to you like an eternity. And learning is easiest for you at this hour too. Youth is the bright sapling that can bend this way or that. By the time you are my age, the wood is set.'

Trees? Saplings? Manchán wondered for a second if his mother wasn't Mothall in disguise and playing a trick on him. You never knew with druids.

'How do I know you're my mother?' he asked suddenly, just to check, and saw by the expression on her face that it must be her.

'For Crom's sake, Manchán,' she snapped, then closed her eyes and pressed her lips together, drawing on her tiny reserves of patience. 'I told your father that this approach wouldn't work,' she muttered, 'but since when has that man ever listened to me?' She opened her eyes again and looked hard at her son.

And now he knew for certain it was her. Nobody he had ever heard of would doubt for a single breath that 'that man' would do exactly what his wife told him. Not even that man himself.

'Manchán,' said his mother, 'I am done talking. You are going to the monastery with my brother and there you will learn music and reading and writing. You will learn about building and animals and crops and anything else the monks have to offer. And why will you do these things?' she asked, and amazingly enough actually waited for him to answer the question.

He knew exactly what he was expected to say. 'To bring honour to the family,' he said sullenly.

'Wrong,' said his mother. 'To bring honour to yourself. It is a different category of thing altogether.'

Manchán was silent. He felt like that hare he had once seen, only without a hole in the wall to escape through this time. Behind him the surface of the river broke, and Muck twitched an ear.

'I'm not going without Muck,' said Manchán.

His mother nodded. 'I've already spoken to my brother about that,' she said, 'and he agrees.'

Well, that was easy, thought Manchán, and wondered what other demand he should make. 'Pagan is allowed visit me,' he said, 'and Méabh isn't. And she can't have my socks.'

'I didn't make them for her,' said his mother.

From the river there came another splash, louder this time. By now it was evening and the long-legged flies were emerging from the green shadows, drawing the fish up to feed.

'Why are you wet?' asked his mother suddenly, and Manchán explained, waiting for her to laugh at him.

Only she didn't. Instead she walked to the river's edge and looked out over the dark glossy surface.

'That must have been some fish,' she said, 'to pull you into the water like that.'

'It was,' said Manchán.

'Do you think it is still there?' asked his mother, and Manchán nodded.

'I think it is over there,' he said, pointing at a spot in the bend where the river deepened and the branches tumbled like hair over the water. 'But it is a hard spot to get to.'

'Most things that are worth doing are hard,' said his mother and bent down to pick up his rod. Then she handed it to him.

'I have no patience for fishing,' she said, 'though I like to eat them. That is what your daddy always said, and he is the man to know. Now show me your skill,' she said, 'while I sit here in the sun, and when you are finished, we will go home to dinner together.'

Honour to the Family

he sun's fire was collapsing in the West and Manchán and his family sat outside their hut watching the spectacle. They had eaten their fill, with enough left over to keep even Muck happy for a while. In a few short days Manchán would be watching the sunset from the monastery on the other side of the lake, and he wasn't looking forward to it, not one little bit. A monk's life was full of rules, everybody knew that, and rules and Manchán just didn't get along, another thing that was widely known. Then Manchán caught Méabh looking at him and said, 'What?'

'They'll never keep you,' said Méabh. 'You'll be back before the solstice.' And she grinned.

'Will you miss me?' asked Manchán.

Méabh said, 'No. Not when I know you'll be back so soon.' She reached across and pinched him on the arm, but gently.

Now Manchán smiled but he rubbed his eyes as well for the turf fire was making them sting. His father cleared his throat and started singing.

Come all you young people
And whisht at my song.
Tis as clear as a bell
And as loud as a gong.
If you heed my advice
Then you'll never go wrong,
And bring honour to the family.

The first is the mother
On that you'll agree.
Bereft of her guidance
Then where would we be?
If you do as she says,
You will make her hap-py.
And bring honour to the family.

'I'm not sure that's a good rhyme,' said Manchán.

'It's a work in progress,' replied his father.

The next is the sister
So gentle and mild,
As soft as an egg
Not properly boiled.
Her heart is so gentle
'Twill never be riled.
She brings honour to the family.

And then comes the father
The last and the least.
His worries are many,
His brow it is creased.
From morning to midnight
He labours unceased,
To bring honour to the family.

'Well,' said their father, 'what do ye think?'

'It's good,' said Méabh. 'The part about me is very accurate.'

'Hmm,' said Manchán's mother.

And Manchán said, 'Isn't there a verse missing?'

'You're right,' said their father, hitting his creased brow.

But the star of the family
The one with the pluck,
Fine-tempered and easy,
Endowed with good luck.
He's the best pig in Ireland
And his name it is Muck.
He brings honour to the family.

'You're joking,' said Manchán.

'I am,' said his father and laughed. He cleared his throat and stood up to sing the last verse as loudly as he could. Everybody in the village heard him.

When I was a young man
I wished for a son,
And I said to your mother
Let's make one.
And now you are here
And this much is clear
You bring honour to our family.

Then he sat back down. In the west the sun was a dull red coal at the edge of everything, and the small family gathered at the spark of their fire was at the centre of the world.

GLOSSARY

BALOR A wicked old god with one good eye
open and one evil, all-blasting eye shut – except
when he unlidded it on his enemies. The ram
called Balor in this story is named after him.

CORACLE A small basket-shaped boat made of
woven branches and covered in greased leather.
The coracle was the forerunner of the currach
and mostly steered with one oar only. It was
often used on lakes and rivers.

CURRACH A long, narrow sea-going boat
beautifully made of split laths and covered in
hide or canvas. The elegant thin oars comple-
mented the lovely slim design. Currachs are
shaped a bit like bananas, though nobody in
Manchán's world would have known this.

DRUIDS The keepers of the old religion, men
with prodigious memories who spent lifetimes

memorising the traditions and knowledge of the land. And because they wrote nothing down, when they were gone, the traditions went with them.

FAIRIES According to many, fairies were the original inhabitants of Ireland, driven underground by our loudness. Others say the less said about them the better. These are a very different kind to the popular image of fairies often found today. Above all, don't annoy them.

FAIRY CIRCLES/RINGS Often formed by mushrooms, sometimes rocks, and widely considered unlucky to tamper with. Why circles (as opposed to squares or triangles) appealed to the fairies has never been explained. Not to be confused with fairy forts, large grassy rings which can still be seen sprinkled all over the country. Another thing not to be tampered with.

GLOSSARY A list of short definitions of words or things in alphabetical order. The verb is 'to gloss', but the phrase 'to gloss over' is also known, especially to Manchán.

HURLEY (OR HURLING) A game played with sticks and a sliotar. Hurling is also called 'the clash of the ash' (see below) – though not in this book.

HURLEY (OR HURLING) STICK The hip-high stick used to play hurling, cut from the ash tree, broadened and flattened at one end. Also known as a 'hurley', 'hurl' or 'camán'.

LAKE FAIRIES As with people, fairies specialise according to location.

LAND OF DREAMS A real place, according to some, but a lot less easy to control than the usual place.

MOTHALL'S GREAT RIVAL He is referring to St Patrick, the man usually considered to be the bringer of Christianity to Ireland. Like many saints, he was famous for his temper, and popularly believed to have driven the snakes from the land. Other explanations have been offered since.

MOTHALL'S PROPHECY All druids specialised in vagueness when it came to prophecies, and Mothall was especially good at this.

'Small armies of ants,' he chanted, 'marching on whiteness, all carrying meaning, and coloured pictures too, lovely to behold. By the hand of the uncle who visits.'

Nowadays, most scholars agree that this probably refers to the illuminated books that monks transcribed onto vellum in the scriptorium of the monastery.

OTHER PEOPLE Another name for the fairies.

PENANCE Acts demonstrating contrition for bad things done, imposed by holy orders.

PÚCA A shape-changing spirit that lives in wild places, like the bog, and often takes on the shape of a galloping black horse.

QUERN A flat, round stone with a wooden handle, used to grind wheat or oats before cooking. A task beyond tedium.

SLÁINTE The Gaelic word for 'health', often uttered, in hope rather than irony, before drinking alcohol.

SLIOTAR (A Gaelic word pronounced 'slither') A small, hard leather ball about the size of a fist, used in the game of hurling. Opinion is divided on whether it is more painful to get hit by a sliotar or a hurley stick.

About the Author and Illustrator

John Chambers was born and raised in Ireland and now lives among the foreigners in another part of the world. He comes and goes sometimes in an aeroplane, a thing not dreamed of by the Druids, or at least if it was, they kept it to themselves. John writes and draws for a living. Had he been born in ancient Ireland he could have ended up illuminating parchments in a monastery. Or fishing, which mightn't have been too bad either. John has three daughters who can all draw better than he could when he was their age. When he writes a story, he reads it to them first.

About the Publisher

Based in Dublin, Little Island Books has been publishing books for children and teenagers since 2010. It is Ireland's only English-language publisher that publishes exclusively for young people. Little Island specialises in publishing new Irish writers and illustrators, and also has a commitment to publishing books in translation.

www.littleisland.ie